THE SATAN SNIPER'S MOTORCYCLE CLUB

NOVELLA

D1519352

Table of Contents

Acknowledgements

Firstly, I would like to say to my kid, that maybe you are too small to read mommas books right now but when you do open it just know, my words are written for you. There is love out there, kiddo. My love for you never dims, never fades, and has no limit.

A huge thank you goes out to Lauren for always making me laugh. Pushing me to finish this book while my life tumbles out of control.

Gary and Swallow who took me on a ride of my life while introducing me to a shit load of bikers. Tyrone for the help with the action scene.

And a thank you to Juan for answering a ton of questions.

And mostly a special thank you to all my email subscribers. You guys inspire me to keep moving, even when I can't get up.

For all of you who search for a keeper.

"She was forgettable, why couldn't I stay away."

For the full experience:[1]

1. <u>Tin man - Miranda Lambert</u>[2]
2. Love me or leave me – Dustin Lynch[3]
3. Jolene – Mylie Cyrus (The backyard session)[4]
4. Ain't no sunshine – Shawn James[5]
5. Chase Rice – Ready Set Roll[6]
6. Halo – Beyonce (Jasmine Thompson version)[7]
7. Florida Georgia Line – H.O.L.Y[8]
8. Chris Stapleton – Tennessee Whiskey[9]
9. Carrie Underwood – Dirty Laundry[10]

---

1. https://www.youtube.com/ playlist?list=PLznsrl4GGTV9k1AnwmcUJl4LQs PXsSwt7

2. https://youtu.be/Y8PWkTnsrCo

3. https://youtu.be/q3O2_J1LT_w

4. https://youtu.be/wOwblaKmyVw

5. https://youtu.be/fIdnpjceg9A

6. https://youtu.be/2a4jXMD-uDI

7. https://youtu.be/wda2qajOBi8

8. https://youtu.be/zXDAYlhdkyg

9. https://youtu.be/4zAThXFOy2c

10. https://youtu.be/lNzHARgbCG8

10. Jonathan Roy – Keeping Me Alive[11]
11. Luke Combs – When it Rains it pours[12]
12. Brett Young – Like I love you[13]
13. Maren Morris – I could use a love song[14]
14. Eli young Band – Crazy Girl[15]
15. Lewis Capaldi – Rush ft. Jessie Reyes[16]
16. Kip Moore – She's mine[17]
17. Ashley McBryde – One night standards[18]

11. https://youtu.be/UyaZmFGyuMg

12. https://youtu.be/uXyxFMbqKYA

13. https://youtu.be/PG2azZM4w4o

14. https://youtu.be/ErdZ_W35xRs

15. https://youtu.be/J3HwFtdVTfM

16. https://youtu.be/0DtxiOAhYdM

17. https://youtu.be/vykhvwCSHj8

18. https://youtu.be/-BXqoGMJUVQ

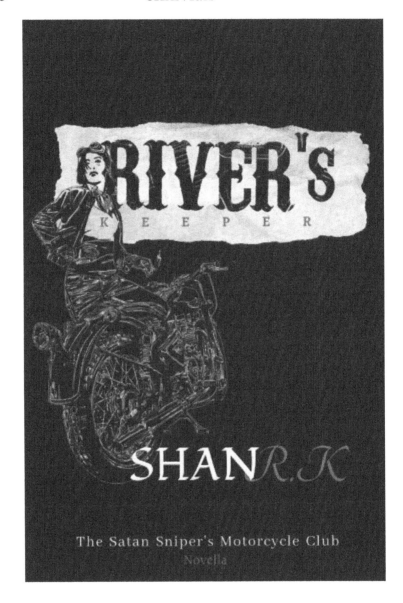

HNNAH

Prelude

Growing up life was good, simple. I took it for granted.

Why not right? I had a stay at home mom and two older brothers. I was the baby and my family treated me as one.

My dad was an electrician for a machine repair company, 10 miles from Laurelhurst, our suburban homestay.

We were never rich, neither were we hurting for cash. I never wore thrift store clothing. Nor did I have to eat the same food two days in a row. Overall life was good.

I know it now, but then I didn't have a clue. Then, life was normal. I never knew things any other way. I was young like that. Naïve.

I attended a public school like most kids in Laurelhurst. Graduating top of my class, I was the first in my family to get accepted into Harvard University. Yes, I was going to do my first-year pre-med. I wanted to be a neurosurgeon. I was ambitious, filled with goals and dreams.

It's amazing how life seems to be going so great, those sleepless nights finally paying off. Because I can tell you, that when you're flying high you feel invincible. I did, and it was the best feeling I ever had.

My brothers attended Washington State, not far from home. Ridge finished his degree in accounting, and Freddy was already a hard-working electrical engineer for a local company. Both my brothers married young. Freddy divorced Celeste a year after they'd tied the knot. He kept insisting she was insane and mom agreed. Freddy had never been happier than the day he signed those papers.

My eldest brother Ridge was six years into his marriage and a proud father of twin girls, Alison and Stacy. Add in a wife that practically took out his socks when he got home from work, Ridge felt like he was king.

He hardly ever came home but mom and dad didn't mind. They believed that no news meant good news. I think they were just tired of having such a noisy house and wanted peace. My parents liked their quiet time.

And me? I was soon to be a student at Harvard. Life was looking up for me. And with my parents who considered the possibility and two brothers who were thrilled I got accepted, I had enough money to pay for the books I needed. It was the only part my scholarship wasn't going to cover.

The world felt touchable and mine for the taking. I was ready to spread my wings and leave my mark on my country. And before I knew it, I was in Cambridge, Massachusetts attending Harvard University.

The first year went on by faster than I thought. I didn't make it home until Christmas. My short breaks were spent studying for extra credits and working at the Sleeve, an upper-class five-star restaurant in the City. I was too exhausted to do anything else.

My personal life was zero to negative one. I was a nineteen-year-old Harvard student with no boyfriend and one friend if I counted my teddy-bear I won at the fair last fall. I wasn't refined enough for the rich kids, not smart enough for the geeks and not serious enough to hang with the other scholarship kids.

It was unacceptable to just be me, I guess. It was the main reason I got the job and focused on my studies.

I believed that if I kept my head on my goals, the time would fly. The thing is, I wasn't paying attention to the other stuff. My mind was focused on my work. That was my first mistake.

My mom always told me that multi-tasking was important, and looking back I should've listened, but I didn't.

Before I knew it, I was in my second year and that was when I got sidetracked.

It was one of those days, where the wind was just wilder than the previous ones. No certainty of what the hours would bring. I always found the air much cleaner and refreshing to smell on campus than the stuffy scent of central city.

Spending time on the grounds whilst I immersed my brain into the complexity of human anatomy was the one pleasure, I allowed myself. And that day was no different. A bit of wind didn't deter me in the slightest.

I had two free periods before I needed to attend a Chemistry class. I was wearing my signature Harvard outfit, comprised of chino pants and a white button-down shirt, completed with a pair of flat nude pumps.

On my first day at Harvard, I arrived in my normal clothes, baggy black Levi jean, black t-shirt paired off with Neon green and pink D&G sneakers. Around my head were my personal styled shocking blue headphones.

I was there for all but ten minutes before I learned that my loose jean and tank tops were not impressing any faculty members. If that wasn't 'message' enough, the next day my bio professor kindly asked me to dress more 'conservative'.

She went as far as letting me out of class early so I could purchase some 'serious clothing'.

Now, a year later and I barely recognized myself.

My maroon framed glasses were the only sign on my body that told people I liked the color, but you didn't hear me complaining. I had a plan, goals.

I was going to be a kick-ass Doctor. Nevermind if I lost a little bit of myself along the way. Who the hell cared if I lost weight and became a shell of the person I once was? So, fucking what, if I was god damn miserable?

I had goals dammit.

Let me tell you the thing about goals, they mean nothing, abso-fucking-lutely nothing if you aren't paying attention to the obstacles because there are always obstacles.

Mine came in a six-foot, two-hundred-pound male named Landon Bennet. He was gorgeous, perfect teeth, perfect hair and a laugh that had me making many mistakes in my life. I met him on the second day of my second year at Harvard.

When I think about how cliché it sounds, saying he was so perfect, so gorgeous, I think of how young and naïve I was back then.

I recall how stupid and foolish I was. He was a junior

partner at a law firm, six-years older than me. And I shit you not, he was my biology professor's brother.

He charmed me within a week, took my virginity in a month and snatched my heart in three. I was a goner for a handsome face and a dazzling smile and in just a year I was Mrs. Hannah Bennet.

In my third year of med-school, my days were spent on Campus and hospitals whilst my nights split into attending Galas or Charity events always ending under Landon.

I failed my third year and Landon insisted I didn't need to work. I should stay at home, he said. Studying wasn't important, I was a kept woman. And like the good wife I was, agreed with him.

That was the second mistake I made. I should've never left Harvard.

My parents were devastated. And my brothers? they didn't even talk to me. That was when I made my third mistake, I cut my family out. I forgot about them, ignored them and eventually, they forgot about me too.

Looking back, I think it was in the third year of our marriage that Landon changed. He wanted a son; I couldn't give it to him.

I wasn't sure why I couldn't fall pregnant. The doctors insisted I was fine. Landon was fine, we were both young fertile people. We had a great sex life, we never used protection, I couldn't understand it.

That should've been my first sign but remember I said I wasn't paying attention. At this stage in my life, I had one goal, pleasing my husband and that was having a baby.

Unfortunately, my husband didn't feel as pleased with me

as I thought. I found this out in our fourth year of marriage when a woman walked up to our door with a baby in her arms claiming it was Landon's son. It was Landon's son.

My husband was cheating on me. Of course, he blamed the entire thing on me. Accusing all of this on me. He said it was my fault because I couldn't fall pregnant, I couldn't give him a son.

After that day I stopped being the good wife, I stopped caring for my husband. Because you see that day, I had a secret of my own, I was pregnant.

I filed for divorce three-weeks later. Landon didn't contest the divorce. He was too wrapped up being a new dad. And I was glad.

If he knew I was carrying his kid I don't think he would've let me go so easy. Then again would he have cared? He let me go without a fight the first time. I don't think adding a baby after he already had one would've changed his mind.

So, there I was, a pregnant twenty-four-year-old divorced, Med-school dropout.

There was no place for me to stay, nothing to fall back on. Not like I could've gone home. My parents were no longer an option for me. I burned those bridges for a man who couldn't keep it in his pants and practically replaced me with an older woman.

I had little to no money in my bank account because when I was getting married, I didn't stop to think about the anti-nuptial contract I signed.

I was too naïve. And let's just say Landon wasn't feeling very generous after I destroyed his house. Technically I didn't blame the guy, I did overdo it.

Throwing a piano out of his window was bound to piss him off. At the time that was the goal, now I was wishing I didn't. Especially since I was going to have to tell him in nine months that we made a baby together.

I wasn't a bad person.

Any man, no matter how much of an asshole he turned out to be, deserved to know his kid. Well, at least be given the chance.

I was hoping Landon wouldn't want that chance.

So pregnant, homeless, and six suitcases full of clothes, shoes, and underwear that wouldn't fit me in five months, it was very light to say my options were limited. I didn't know much about what I was going to do, but like always I had a plan, and this time I was finally paying attention.

I was going to move to a small place, where nobody knew Landon Bennet, the famous Mercantile Attorney. I wanted a place where I could just live. Somewhere safe for my baby, cheap for my pocket and far from this City.

A small town. The good thing about America is we had those in spades. There were small towns everywhere. Fewer people, quiet places, perfect for me, safe for my baby.

Choosing a place was the easy part, but getting a job proved tricky. I traveled to Texas and stopped in town after town. I applied for different jobs and when I didn't get a call back, I moved on.

By the time I finally found my new home, I had sold my jewelry, and pawned five pairs of Jimmy Choo shoes. I had around three hundred dollars in my bank account from living wisely and was eighteen weeks pregnant with my daughter, Jocelyn May Evans the second.

I was also the newest medical secretary for the Med-life hospital in a small town called Kanla. My income would be good enough to rent a small apartment on the outer part of the residential area and support my baby. It was going to be tight, but we'd get by.

That was my goal. I was paying attention and thinking about the bigger picture. I was finally multitasking because I didn't have a choice. I, Hannah Evans was a single, pregnant woman in a new town.

It was scary starting a life on my own and then bringing a child into the mix. But pray and behold, after fifteen hours of labor pains and an emergency c-section later, on July 15th Jocelyn May Evans the second was born.

I was a mother and for the first time in years I didn't feel lost, I didn't feel unwanted, I wasn't alone anymore. I was the mother of a healthy baby girl. It was then that I decided that the only goal I would ever have was to be the best mother I could be and lord did I try.

HANNAH

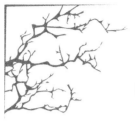

Chapter 1

6 *years later*

"Jo come on, we gonna be late," I scream from inside where

I'm currently standing by the small kitchen window watching

my little girl chasing Kim McGerby's son around the small

complex where we stay. Well used to stay.

After five years of saving all my quarters, doing double shifts and working part-time for my friend DJ

I've finally managed to put a down payment on a small two-bedroom house in the center of Kanla.

It's down the road from the diner and local church, barely a couple of miles from work and most importantly it's near my best friend DJ's house.

It isn't a prime location, but then again this is Kanla, there is none. But the place is mine, well as mine as it can be until I paid off the mortgage.

Jocelyn has been so excited about the new place, having her own room and a yard but all I've been doing is stressing. And with barely two days to settle in before work Monday morning and that includes today there isn't time for anything else.

My bestie DJ owns the local club just past the mall about five miles north from the hospital where I work.

She couldn't close shop today and I didn't expect her to, especially when it was the busiest day of the month. She offered to help me out tomorrow morning but I never miss church so I ended up taking my co-workers up on their standing offer to come in today and help me unpack.

There is no way I'm going to be able to swing it on my own.

Jocelyn's light brown locks swish down her back, looking golden under the bright Southern sun as she runs inside.

My head shakes in amazement as I watch my little hero. Her long legs carry her closer to me, before a pair of light grey eyes so much like my own find me staring. Her small button nose scrunches up right before she blesses me with one of her goofy smiles and rolls her eyes.

"You've got practice in fifteen minutes. Get your shoes on missy."

She scowls, as her nose wrinkles, a telltale sign that I'm not going to like what my six-year-old kid is about to say,

"I told you I ain't no missy momma. Missy is Jamie Coleman's sister and I ain't her, she stinks like rotten fish, I saw her yesterday down by the field and she looked like she didn't bathe for days, Caden said if we went close to her we might catch somethin', is it true momma?"

"Jocelyn May, didn't I tell you not to bad mouth that girl."

"I ain't bad-mouthing her, I was just..." she argues back at the same time her posture straightens in defense.

"Just what Jo?" I interrupt in my sternest voice, my eyes firmly placed on hers.

We stay like this, in a standoff until she relents. Her shoulders hunch and she huffs with a slight frown still marring her brows,

"Nothing momma."

"That's what I thought, that girl has enough to worry about without you and your friends adding to that." I don't like this part of parenting, and there was a time when I didn't do it but my baby got out of hand when she pushed a kid off a swing last year.

I was called into the pre-school and ended up taking Jocelyn out and transferring her to the local public school even though I knew she wasn't entirely to blame. The boy she pushed played a part too, the only difference was that Jo was the first one to strike.

At the time I didn't know how to handle this. I wasn't keen on spanking my kid and punishing her seemed a bit harsh. Talking to her didn't work either because my baby even at five had a temper. So, becoming stern and strict was my go-to evil, but a necessary one at that. Lord knew that if I didn't play the bad parent game with my kid what my baby would turn out like.

But it doesn't mean I like it, my mother never told me how hard it was to be a mother, she made it look easy. It's the most difficult position a person can have.

When you got a determined kid like Jocelyn staring at you

hunched and sorrowful, it's even worse. Because even though I'm aware that deep down she doesn't see the error of her ways I just got to go mush.

It's like a curse because instead of letting Jo pass me like the strict parent I'm ought to be, I snatch her around the belly and tickle her something crazy.

She howls, "Momma, I'm gonna pee my panties."

My big smile matches hers as I let her go, 'cause now I'm feeling lighter. Watching her rush off to our old room where I still have a few suitcases scattered on the floor that needs to be taken over to our new place, my moment of happiness is short-lived. Truth is it's hard as a parent as is, but a single one? I have no clue how I've done it for these past six-years.

My hat comes off for those single parents with two or more kids just doing it on their own.

But isn't that what loving our kids is about? Sacrifice, selflessness, love, devotion. It's so close to marriage vows, difference is, being a parent isn't tied by empty promises, and repeated words.

To be a parent is to be bound by blood, it's a lifetime commitment.

Because, no matter where you are, or where your kid is, the day that child sucked its first breath was the day you became bound.

I am no perfect mother, but I have made sacrifices.

One of them was staying in this one-bedroom complex since I stepped foot in Kanla almost six years ago.

At one time it was enough for the two of us, but my girl is tall and she needs her own space. I thought about this when Jo was a year old and was getting bigger and fast. She is one of the tallest in her class and a purebred tomboy.

Hence why I'm taking her to soccer practice on a Saturday morning and not to dance lessons like most of the girls in Kanla. But Jocelyn has never been anything but unique.

"Momma let's go I'm done."

Her grey eyes shoot up, and my heart swells with a heaviness I've always blamed on my past because she looks just like her father when she does that even with eyes and curly light brown hair so much like my own.

Too bad he will never know that.

Six-years-ago I kept my word and emailed Landon a picture of a one-week old Jocelyn and a note that it was his.

I promised myself, I wouldn't recall the email he sent me back unless I had to. But I will just say that he wanted nothing to do with his daughter.

I didn't cry as I should've, I guess a part of me knew that it would be a possibility even though it hurt. I did love the man once, I mean I married him, gave up Harvard for him.

Didn't it count for something? Apparently not.

He didn't even have the decency to send me a parting check or offer to pay child support.

It would've been nice if he could've helped me pay for at least one pack of diapers or sat with me on one of those sleepless nights when she suffered from colic but whatever.

I had no regrets because I wasn't looking over my back waiting for him to come and take her away these past six-years. Jocelyn might be fatherless but she has me.

She is my kid; all mine and I like not having to share her with anybody else. I'm selfish like that.

"Please put your seatbelt on, I'm not getting stopped today by Sheriff Briggs 'cause you can't sit still," I say as I open the back door of my small white Camry knowing I'm going to be shouting at her about the same thing until we get to soccer practice.

Lucky, I have a safe ride.

The car is something I bought off DJ a few years back. It was a newer model at the time and she allowed me to pay her off over the past three years, interest-free.

Which worked out well because there was no way I could afford something so nice otherwise. But that's the thing about Kanla, the people are either your friends and they're all in or they aren't.

There's no grey areas and no shady characters. Well, at least not anymore.

Three-years back, a drug ring came around our small town. In the beginning, a lot of the youngsters got hooked on drugs.

And the thrill of hanging with the gangster group was the weekend rush.

That was until someone ended up dead and it wasn't from an overdose.

No, more like cold-blooded murder.

After that, things got very bad.

The gangsters started robbing our stores and pushing people around, there were even incidences of rape.

I wasn't sure who it was but somebody around here knew a biker club and next thing we knew these scary men and women were riding on motorcycles and taking residence in our town.

They wore sleeveless jackets with lots of different color patches in the front and a logo on the back that was meant to scare everybody and called themselves The Satan Sniper's Motorcycle Club.

The motorcycle club pushed the gangsters out and kept any riff-raff from entering Kanla since.

The bikers never really kept to themselves. From the first day they rode into town, it was never a secret that they lived here. Some of them have since opened businesses.

Others were building properties, hiring locals and creating more job opportunities for our residents. A few of them even volunteer around the town.

They protect our small population and in return, we adopt a don't ask don't tell policy. We all know they are a group of Ex-snipers and soldiers who still work for the government.

We aren't sure what they do in that farmhouse all the time but I heard rumors that I'm not too keen on confirming its authenticity.

The finer details are something I am still not sure of because it isn't my business but like all the folks in Kanla, I'm just glad to have them around.

I was so close to skipping this small place when the drug gang moved to town because as much as I love Kanla I love Jocelyn much more and if it wasn't for The Satan Snipers, I'm not sure what I would've done.

I double-check to make sure my kid is buckled up in the back. No matter how many times I'm going to 'remind' Jo to put her seatbelt back on, there is no way I'm starting this car until I know I have at least made sure she's strapped up when we leave.

Once my sunglasses are on my eyes, I take the

thirty-minute drive in stride, and pass the park and then The Satan Snipers Clubhouse before finally getting to the school.

This, however, doesn't happen without me telling Jo a million times to put her seatbelt on because I'm driving.

Lucky enough I don't get stopped by that jackass Sheriff Briggs. The man still thinks I'm going to go on a date with him.

Stepping out of the car with my black converse and shorts I lastly realize I forgot to change my black t-shirt which is full of bleach stains from the cleaning I was doing this morning. I open the door for Jo and she hops out.

Her eyes rooted toward the field in front of us that I know is full of boys and fathers. The Sun's bright rays have me squinting when I slip off my shades.

"Momma can I go now?" Jo asks me in a hurried voice, anxious as ever to see her friends.

I look down at her outfit to make sure she's good. Her white shorts have a bit of a stain but either than that her white t-shirt is clean, hair neat but still open and big frown plastered on her face is all normal when she's antsy.

"You good to go, baby, no pushing today alright, can I get a kiss," I say as I pinch her cheek.

"Momma, Caden's watchin'."

I roll my eyes, and make a sad face,

"Okay then, maybe later?"

She looks back to the field before her vision finds mine.

"Maybe a quick one."

After a very quick kiss, I watch Jo rush off onto the other side of the fence. The shiny new fence surrounding the school's property is just one of the new things The Satan Snipers have done to improve our small town.

The motorcycle club also bought two school buses for the local high school last year when the school's one blew up because it was so old.

Barry Keager, the town drunk was the only one who got hurt. He sustained multiple injuries but nothing severe enough for him to put the bottle down.

He is one lucky bastard but then I always wondered what the hell was he doing around the parked school bus in the first place.

I stand on the outside of the fence and watch Jo from my vantage point as she dribbles the ball. I'm not going to embarrass my kid and walk down there dressed as I am, but I'm not missing a single game either.

I can't afford luxuries like that without it affecting my kid because I'm a single mother. I am also subsequently a father too.

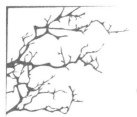

Chapter 2

The brown glass body of the beer I've been nursing for way longer than I'd like sweats as it slowly loses its cool. The Italian fucker tied to the plastic chair that's positioned in the middle of the lounge area with a black bed sheet acting as a floor rug sweats as he loses more blood.

A few days ago, I was on my way to Idaho looking for a lead on my latest assignment. Today I'm in the last place that I want to be in.

I am back home, in good ole' Kanla. I knew I had to return to it all eventually, never thought that day will be anytime soon.

It's an easy seven years since I've been back and while the people are the same the place looks different.

I expected old feelings of guilt to return but there was nothing but anger and determination. A lot of it had to do with the reason I was even in Kanla.

Just thinking about the whole thing almost has me laughing while watching this waste of space bleed.

When I arrived a few hours after a clipped word from our National President, Ribs, to haul ass to Kanla, my first thoughts were the fucking cartel.

I sent my brothers to Kanla a few years ago when the Mexican Cartel tried to take the town and use it for a dumping ground.

I was still stationed in C.I.U in Korea and I couldn't just come back then. Not that I wanted to either but I would've if I could, especially after the call from my cousin Daisy Jane.

But now things are different because for the past year I've been a retired agent of the government and a full-time National Sergeant-at-arms for The Satan Snipers.

I am also the go-to guy the club uses for intense interrogation since I've done it for twelve years while serving my country.

So, there I was hauling ass to Kanla thinking about all the ways I was going to torture the Cartel for fucking with my home town again.

Imagine my surprise when this entire full fuck fest turns out to be because of a homeless chick named Beggar, who is a wanted murderer that single-handedly took out eighteen of our men.

I didn't believe it at first but after I watched the footage a couple of dozen times while I ripped myself to shreds almost every one of those times, it finally sank in.

Now here we are searching for this girl, and the guy naked on the chair I'm currently looking at is our biggest lead we had in the last three-weeks since Beggar left.

"Let's try this one more time." I shrug out of my cut and stare calmly at him.

He inspects my actions from a pair of swollen, purplish, red eyes. Well, what's left of it. I think Killer left lasting damage to the Italians left eye socket.

It's starting to get black.

"Where is Beggar?" My question sounds nonchalant but this fucker has been sitting in that chair for the past three or so hours.

The house is empty besides the two of us. My Kanla brothers and the women are volunteering at the local church today. I could've joined them and handled this guy another day but I'm not ready to be known yet without facing the reason I left Kanla in the first place.

The woman I left behind, Lauren Cormack.

The Italian spits out a broken tooth and blood right as my boots meet the black sheet.

"You know," I tell him, "you got a great pair of balls. You would've made an excellent brother, too bad you on the wrong side of the pavement."

I tut as he bucks, flicking open my switchblade dangling it in front of his face,

"Now, let's try that again, only this time without the attitude. Where is Beggar?"

"I told you cunt, I don't fuckin' aaaahhhh, you, aaaahhh," He screams like a fuckin' porn chick on heat.

I take pride as I stab him with my switchblade twice in the left thigh and once in the left shoulder.

I don't go deeper than one centimeter. I've been doing all kinds of creative art to this guy's body and I know the fucker isn't going to be singing.

Straightening to my full height I look detached as I ask him something my National Prez wants to know.

"Is Beggar safe?"

His shoulders hunch when his blood-smeared chest rises and falls rapidly as his body begins to shake with tears while his head swings from left to right.

He knows what comes next, he has proved not worthy to me, not worthy to my club. It takes him a minute before he can control himself enough to be coherent.

"No, that girl should've nev...ah..never ga..ga...given herself up," he coughs up blood as he continues without looking at me,

"As soon as he finds his daughter, Lucca plans to take his wife and child to his small island off New Orleans. Lucca is obsessed with her; he will never let her leave him again."

I stand still, my arms crossed over my chest, as the man finds his words,

"The last time I saw Beggar, he was putting a shock collar around her neck."

He sniffs.

"She only gave herself up to protect those girls man. He asked why did she change her mind, she told him rather a familiar..." I slice the blade across his neck, granting him a quick death.

"Rather a familiar monster than an unfamiliar friend," The deep voice which finishes that sentence is the only sound the ghost makes as he enters the room.

"Got bored playing holy arth thou?" I ask without turning to face him as I stare at the now vacant body. I say a silent prayer and close the Italians eyes before I slide my bloody blade across my leather pants.

"It's Sunday," he points out, "gotta phone my sisters." With that, I feel his retreat as his dangerous aura leaves the room with him.

I've known Killer since he joined the special ops program a few years back. I was the one who introduced him and Snake to the biker world.

They were both lost, neither of them fitting in with their blood relatives. They had no specific place to call home, a place where they wouldn't be judged, where they could be free. A place they could call their home.

I never recruited many in The Satan Snipers although I've been in the club since I turned nineteen. I joined two weeks before my first tour. Never looked back since, and neither has Killer. The boys' position in the club is under wraps for now. Very few people know his rank in the club. It was orders from my Prez, and the few who know won't go back on their word.

It's for the best.

Thing is, there's a snitch in our club and has been for a while. If anyone could sniff him out it'll be Killer.

You never see the ghost coming until it's going through you, 'cause it always strikes from the back and it doesn't do it 'cause it's a coward it does it because it follows no fucking rules.

HANNAH

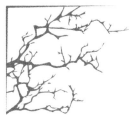

Chapter 3

Two weeks in our new place and it's finally feeling like home. Jo has been spending even more time with Caden since he stays a few doors down while I spend more time on my studying.

As grateful as I am for the job I have, the Lord knows I don't like it. I need something challenging, which is why I'm finishing off med-school part-time.

It isn't easy, but I have enough credits to do it. Add in the Harvard letter I received a few years ago when I decided to go down this road, I'm finally able to complete my four years. It would take me another six years until I'm done, but I'm okay with that.

I have nowhere to go, and I'm in no rush to finish it, well, not much of one. It'll be nice to make more money and not have to worry about counting my quarters for once.

I'm sitting by the black plastic coffee table outside with the floral umbrella stuck in the center. My notes lay scattered on the table, while my chipped coffee cup stands to the side, where a bee currently buzzes about.

Jo and Caden are running around the house, chasing each other. It's one of those days when the sun is just there, and the heat isn't going to get better, nor is this bee harassing my cold coffee.

Groaning as a big sigh leaves my mouth and my stiff neck protests my movement, I get up from the plastic chair I'm sitting on. It's so hot that my white dress is sticking to the back of my thighs.

I tug on the fabric until it's properly in place, aware that I probably have a wet spot on the rear of my dress, but don't care much to change it and head on inside to the kitchen.

Today I marked as my day of studying, I wasn't wearing makeup, and my shoes didn't consist of a pair of four-inch heels.

Nope, I'm in a couple of two-dollar red beach tongs I got from the local people's market, the town hosts every 4th of July. My hair isn't blown out. Instead, it's in a messy high knot on top of my head, and I couldn't be bothered. I won't say I look bad, but I don't look like I made an effort either.

Today's my day off, I have no shopping, and definitely, no man to dress up for, and even if I did, there's no way I'm doing it in this darn heat.

I'm thinking all this as I trot my sticky, sweaty body into my kitchen.

I pull the freezer key from the top of the white, old rusty refrigerator that has been dying a slow, painful death since I bought it seven years ago.

I couldn't afford a new one then and certainly can't afford

a new one now. I open the freezer, which I keep stacked with Popsicles and ice-cream, hence why I keep it locked from Jo. Taking two red Popsicles out for the kids, I head on outside.

Walking around the white and brick surfaced house, my smile drops from my face.

"Jo, Caden," I call out.

They seem too quiet all of a sudden, that is so far from a good sign when you put those two together in the same sentence, it's troubling.

The sound of motorbikes coming up the street isn't anything unusual, and I ignore it as I have for the past two weeks since I've moved in.

Ricky's local supermarket is up the road from our home, and the bikers go there often just like most folks in our small town.

Rounding the corner, I spot two bikers in front of my house, watching Jo kick the one biker's motorcycle.

I see the error of my ways and also the temper of my daughter.

Mindful of the other small group of bikers driving past us without slowing down, I don't look too closely at the two Satan Snipers stationed in front of my house.

I rush over to pull Jo way.

"Jo, stop it," I yell in my sternest voice I can manage, considering I'm nervous and a tiny bit scared.

"You had no business killin' it, now he's dead," She screams at them, and I can hear the tears in my girl's voice.

My eyes instantly go to the ground spotting the squashed frog.

I cringe, *poor Grogg*.

"You killers, I wish someone smashed you under a bike," Jo yells loud enough to inform the entire neighborhood.

"Jo, that's enough," I say in a quiet but firm voice pulling her closer toward me with the Popsicles still clutched in my hand.

She doesn't listen to me, and I'm winded when she elbows me by mistake (I hope) and forces me to let her go as I drop the Popsicles on the ground.

My kid doesn't go kicking the bike again but stands there with her arms folded and a big angry scowl on her tear-filled face, and I see this as I bend my head looking at her instead of the two men.

The heat is scorching, and I'm tempted to pick up the Popsicles I dropped on the ground and shove it between my breasts.

But I don't think it'll be appropriate behavior with the men who are both off their bikes watching my girl and Caden.

He is standing a few feet in front of Jo with his arms folded across his small chest. *So, protective.*

"Where's your dad, kid?" The deep gravel voice has me looking up into the sunglass covered gaze of the biker talking.

My eyes don't wander below his chest even though I want to.

He's about six-two, broad-chested with a grey t-shirt covered with a sleeveless biker jacket that's decorated with numerous colored badges.

His chin has a small indent that is noticeable under the short scruff of hair surrounding the bottom half of his face.

"With his other family." That stops me dead in my tracks from looking any further or deeper at him or the other silent statue biker behind him.

I straighten my shoulders and grab my kid and Caden loosely around their necks.

"I'm sorry about my kid, but you crushed her frog," I say incomplete defense to my kid's actions.

Yes, I am that mother.

Jo is quiet, which I'm glad for, 'cause I know that question hurt her something fierce, and when my kid is hurt, she typically lashes out.

"Sorry 'bout your frog kid. Swear I didn't see it. If there's anything I could do lemme know."

I start to shake my head, refusing when he lifts his hand. His index finger shakes, shushing me at the same time he's bending down and taking his glasses off.

My god, the guy has gorgeous light blue eyes that don't waiver from my girl.

"There must be somethin' you want?"

He emphasizes the word somethin', with a slight southern drawl. I'll never admit it, but my heart does weird things.

I'm getting a funny feeling that I have long since forgotten how to have.

I'm not comfortable any longer. I'm aware of my messy hair, sticky skin, and thin dress.

Yet, the biker hasn't looked away from Jo.

I'm almost invisible. Staring at this man, a second more is going to make me seem like a hussy. I know this.

Yet, I don't stop looking until Caden bends his head over to Jo.

Caden whispers in Jo's ear while I stand there a bit helpless, a lot stunned, and extremely flustered.

Damn, it's so darn hot.

"There is one thing." It's the tone of Jo's voice that has me dreading this conversation that will follow my daughters' request.

"Okay, shoot."

Jo steps a few feet forward stopping in between his thick thighs, and leaves me stunned when she sits her bottoms on his right leg.

I expect him to fall since he is balancing on his haunches, but he maintains a solid form from his boot covered feet.

It's silly, but I'm impressed.

Jo whispers in his ear.

I watch his eyes crease up on the sides as his cheeks pull taut into a big close-mouthed smile. The biker is a good-looking guy, but dangerous. Someone I should stay away from.

"Hah, you gonna make me pay for that frog aren't you, he must've been one hell of a pet, but I did say anything. I guess I'll be seeing you bright and early tomorrow."

She hops off the biker's leg and steps back, right into my clutches as he stands up.

He doesn't extend his hand when his blue gaze focuses on me.

"You must be Hannah, Daisy Jane told me alota 'bout you," He says this as he peruses my body without making it too visible but noticeable enough to get his point across.

This biker is definitely checking me out in front of my kid.

"Well, that's just great for me and a shame for you because she never mentioned you," I point out straight-faced.

Eyes narrowing, he stands there staring at me, not saying

a thing. Ring covered fingers lift to rub aimlessly on the dark scruff of his jaw when I don't drop my own.

What will it be like to touch a rough chiseled face like his? It has been a while since I've felt a man's rough skin against my fingertips.

There's no reason why I deprive myself of something I could have so quickly. Maybe it's because I had it, and I allowed myself to get sidetracked by it.

Or solely because I spent so many years trying to please a man that didn't want me. Truth is, there is no reason, I had sex with two guys after Landon. I felt nothing then as I opened my legs to those men.

Yet, as I look at the biker who remains staring at me as if I am some casual girl, he would forget come tomorrow morning, I feel more, so much more than when I reached a climax at the end of a meaningless one nightstand.

I know nothing about this man; besides a simple fact, he brings a whole new definition to the word rough.

I'd be a fool to not notice the golden tones of his skin that once upon a time turned deep shades of red after a few minutes in the Southern sun, but has long since lost its virgin glow.

Now, his flesh, marked by years under the sun, scarred by paths of his life and aged by the outcome of his choices.

"Knowing Daisy Jane, I bet she didn't," He muse's way too loud, "Might wanna remember the heads up I gave ya."

"Huh?" My voice sounds as surprised as I feel.

"What heads up?"

My girl starts twisting her neck, and I hold on a bit tighter. Thankful, my eyes are shielded by the big tree a few feet away from the motorbikes 'cause I don't have to move my hands from Caden and Jo and risk my kid running back to the biker.

I'm not sure how that makes me feel.

"That I'll be stayin' next door for a coupla weeks," His deep voice states in a matter-of-fact.

"Might wanna ask Daisy Jane 'bout me then, seein' as we gonna be neighbors and all." The tug on the right side of his mouth doesn't go unnoticed, and I find my gaze fixed on his sensual lips instead of what comes out of it.

Why do I have to be attracted to an asshole? Didn't my body learn its lesson?

Doesn't it know an asshole when it sees one?

"Momma, can Caden and I go change the Popsicles?" Jo interrupts my drooling. I bend my head, staring into her pleading gaze.

I reluctantly let the two of them go, and they don't waste time running into the house, *traitors*.

Once I see they're inside, I turn back to look at the biker and see the silent biker he was with is now across the road.

I swear the guy was right there seconds ago. I shake my head at how I didn't even notice the biker crossing the street.

I'm usually an observant person, more so after Jo was born, but I also have to admit that I wasn't always that observant.

I didn't notice when Landon was banging a woman ten years older than me. I didn't pay attention when I was signing an anti-nuptial agreement that screwed me over in the end.

When I practically gave up my entire family for a man who couldn't even keep it in his pants long enough to get home? I wasn't even thinking then.

The only thing I observed was my cycles and how great my

sex life needed to be, so my husband didn't get bored while he planted his seed in me.

I will never make that mistake.

"Never again," I mumble, knowing that it's a lie as I digest what the biker standing in front of me just said before Jo and Caden left.

As I do this, my insides twist and the flesh beneath my skin tingles, making me want to rip the top part out and inflict pain because it feels way too good. And we all know what happened the last time I felt remotely good.

Not to say that I would've walked a different path, Jesus is my witness that I wouldn't.

I walked through the tunnel and saw the light when I stared into my baby's eyes for the first time. Doesn't mean I'm going to walk through it again. I already have enough light.

I'm not feeling greedy enough to want more, then I'll just be asking to get burned. And this hot biker staring at me with nothing more than a keen interest of a one-night stand will burn me so bad I'll never see the light, even once I'm out of the tunnel.

"I'll be sure to get all the nitty grits about my new neighbor biker-guy the next time I see Daisy Jane. Guess I'll be seein' you around then."

I'm proud of myself for keeping this conversation short when my body is wanting to have all kinds of long talks with this biker.

He has a charming smile; I see this when his cheeks stretch taut. A small, barely noticeable dimple pops up on the left side. His face lights up as I wait for the courtesy goodbye.

"River," He says, and again, I'm like,

"Huh?"

"My name, it's River."

"Really?" I widen my eyes as a look of disbelief paints my face.

"Really. You got a problem with my name Hannah Banana?"

"Not you too," I groan.

"Name made sense after I watched your ten-second video, quite a show there."

"You lie," I say, already knowing that he most certainly did. He doesn't say a thing.

Taking a deep breath of hot air, I try hard to compose myself as I declare,

"I'm going to kill DJ."

The low chuckle coming from his throat brings nervous flutters that tickle me in welcomed places.

My stomach turns with knowledge that this hot, dangerous biker knows something so stupid, yet personal about me. River has heard and seen way too much about me. Standing outside my house leaning in toward me, his feet stretches open. Muscular arms cross over his chest like he plans to hold his position all day talking to me. So close, but too far.

It's then I register something I didn't think about. What is he doing in front of my property in the first place?

River's sight tracks behind me, and I don't have to turn around to know he is staring at Jo and Caden. Shaking his head with a speculative stare that I'm sure will make any weaker man tremble. Lucky for me, I'm not a man, nor am I weak.

"You have one hell-of-a kid there. Might wanna keep her temper under control, though. Abusing strangers bikes in the middle of Kanla or anywhere else is dangerous. It ain't gonna earn her any brownie points with the locals."

I wisely choose to ignore the 'locals' comment and focus on the rest as I glare at him, all pleasantries forgotten,

"Are you insulting my kid?" I'm aware my loud voice has dropped, and the calm façade is now in its place.

River's face goes from relaxed to defensive in seconds.

"Fuck no, I was giving you advice."

"It didn't sound like advice, I'm pretty sure it was an insult." I know my face is all sticky and my hairline too.

Also, I probably look like a sick freckled tomato, but I still scowl at him.

River's blue eyes narrow as his teeth lock, his jaw flexing in obvious irritation. Hah, it looks like his true nature is coming out to play. Too bad I got no time for games. I'm about to say just that when he bellows,

"Why would I insult her when I agreed to build her a fuckin' treehouse that's going to put me back a coupla grand? I didn't come here to listen to your bitchin' Hannah."

"You did what?" I know I'm screeching, and Ms. Drew is going to come outside and explain to me again the 'correct' behavior of a good Christian woman.

Thing is, right now, I'm livid.

Who the hell is this guy to think he can just promise my daughter a freaking treehouse without even consulting me?

He crosses his big beefy arms over his broad chest and leans on the middle part of his blue and black motorcycle. Something works behind his cold depths that stay directed straight on me.

"Don't bitch about the treehouse, 'cause I'm doing it. I said I will, and I don't lie to kids."

I think this over as my left arm burns from the sun's hot rays.

I was going to give him shit, but his reasons are good ones. I'm a single mother. There is no way I'll ever be able to afford a treehouse, especially now with a mortgage that's much higher than the rent I was paying before.

I didn't get into Harvard for being a pretty face. I know a good thing when I see it.

And a treehouse for my kid, is something Jo has wanted forever.

I would never be able to give her that. This a great thing.

"Fine, if you want to spend your money on my kid, I'm not stopping you, knock yourself out, and I mean really KNOCK yourself out."

He stands there in front of me so quiet and still, that I begin to squirm with how uncomfortable and flushed I feel with this man's heated attention directed only on me.

"Go out with me."

"What?!" I yelp barely missing a beat.

"Go out with me." He repeats his statement, tense shoulders belying his casual pose.

"Seriously, What?" My mouth gaps open, and I'm positive I resemble some animal that just realizes it's been trapped in big bright headlights.

He killed Grogg, insulted Jo, then bribed her with a treehouse, which I'm not complaining about, yes, but I'm not thrilled about either, far from it.

I would never be able to give her that, and I know he knows

that, but still, he expects me to just go on a date with him? Is the guy a wacko?

"Yup." I'm startled by the sound of the deep and smooth voice coming from the biker that was across the road a minute ago.

He has somehow managed to stroll over to retake his place without me knowing.

And judging by his word, also now fully aware that I just called River a wacko, loud.

I don't retract it when the quiet one confirms the obvious. River, my new neighbor, is crazy.

I'm going to be living next to a crazy person. A hot and sexy crazy male who wants to go out with me.

My focus switches to the young silent biker. Dressed in the clubs biker jacket that isn't sleeveless like the one River is wearing nor is it filled with numerous badges, he is a sight for eyes.

He has only one with a single word written, SOLDIER. I drop my vision, but not before I notice the perfect, clean-shaven angles of his face or the length of his neck. His leather pants are new and fit him perfectly, hinting at the lean muscle behind his clothing.

"Stop checking Killer out when I'm standing right here." My eyes snap back to the big and imposing River.

The hint of irritation in his voice doesn't go unnoticed.

"Who voted you so important to think that I give a dime that you're standing right there or even consider going out with you? No one that's who, you wanna know why?"

His lips twitch, thinning as he shakes his head in the negative.

"Well, I'll tell you anyway, it's because you and I in the same sentence are never going to happen," I inform him of this even though I know that I want it to.

River's neck extends, head bent slightly to the left, tilted away from the sun. The long column of his exposed throat now on full display. I know I shouldn't like the biker. He's more trouble than humble, but dammit, he is a fine piece of meat.

I would never call him gorgeous 'cause he and that ship never met, but I would put him in the V.I.P of the bad boy cruiseline. I've never had dangerous before.

"Come on, Hannah, just admit that you want to." Arrogance and certainty come off him in waves.

"No, I don't," I snort.

River purposely blinking eyes call my words shit. *Arrogant prick.*

"Baby, you've been askin' for it since you came trotting those sexy legs over here. And then screamin' for it when you blushed fifteen fucking shades of red when I asked you out and now look at you. You can't even keep still, can you? Tell me something, Hannah banana."

"What?" My arms cross under my braless breasts, as blunt fingers dig into my rib cage as I swallow hard.

I'm not liking where this conversation is going. I know when I'm getting in too deep, and this conversation is going into dark and unknown territory. I sum up enough courage to look the biker straight in his eyes.

The glint in his heated stare can be seen from the few feet of space between him and I.

Following his hot look is awareness and simple fact, I'm the only one blinded by unknown territory.

River knows precisely where he is steering me, and like any naïve woman that has gotten in his sights even if it's just for a night, I walked right into it.

"How long since you've been fucked? I'm betting it's been a hell of a long fuckin' time, hasn't it?" Boy does his words confirm it.

I know my mouth gaps open, I feel it. I have to close it and open then close it again before I scowl. I'm not only affronted, but the blush creeping up my neck is the exact answer this arrogant and way too knowledgeable biker wants to hear.

It's a shameful thing admitting to myself that I haven't been fucked in a long time. The truth is, after Landon, no guy has held my interest beyond a day. Those days were two, one with Raine Donovan, the local hot chef. He was my poor attempt at a relationship.

When my colleague, Lisle Donelly, who might I add is fifty-eight, stated that she was getting fucked four times a week, I needed to know if I still had what it took.

It didn't end well.

Nearly a year and a half after that was the town playboy Deputy Gregory Deane, Kanla's deputy sheriff.

He wasn't anything to sneeze about, blond hair, light brown eyes with a rippled six-pack was something women drooled over alone, add in the badge, and who could blame me? Both men wanted more, but I wasn't even remotely interested.

They were too gentle for my tastes, neither fucked me, just treated me like something easily broken, soft, and sweet. I didn't mind soft but sweet, and I never really seen eye to eye.

Landon, on the other side, well, I loved sex with Landon.

He was the best man by far that I have ever been with. I never got bored in my brief marriage, nor did he ever leave me unsatisfied. I wasn't even aware that women could also fake an orgasm during that period of my life.

I only found that out when I started working for DJ. Well, I found out all kinds of things working at The Lick night club.

For instance, a big sexy biker like River will more than be able to measure up to any man. The only difference between the two will be River will easily walk away.

There will be no room for anything permanent, well not from a thirty-year-old single parent with stretch marks on her ass and belly.

"I am going to pretend you didn't just ask me that." My voice hitches in the end, and I'm not even sure why.

"Jake Stiles, is that you?" I turn around at the soft voice of Lauren Anderson coming from next door.

The girl is like two years younger than me, but she looks a lot less than twenty-seven in her denim shorts and a white tank top.

She is the town's beauty, and though I haven't lived here my whole life, everyone in town knows about Jake Stiles and the vision he left behind, Lauren Anderson.

They are one of the 'it' couples in Kanla, 'they were meant to be' is what most folks around here always say when the two are brought up in conversation.

Which is usually when Lauren is in earshot to hear the whole thing. I feel sorry for her, she seems lost and so sad.

Question is why did he leave? Who would leave a girl like Lauren behind?. No one knows why the guy left Kanla, but he hasn't been back for years. But he is back now.

I watch River, who is staring at Lauren, stunned, speechless, and I see the love in his eyes for the girl. She is his, and he still belongs to her. It's now that I know I should get going.

A small smile creeps up on me at how laughable this is. River just asked me out.

For a second, I considered going. I'm a thirty-year-old divorced single mother, no way am I even on the radar.

I'm not a plain Jane. I can't even think that, because Jo looks so much like me. My kid is gorgeous, calling myself anything dull will be insulting my kid. And I know it will be a lie.

I never disliked what I saw in the mirror, even when my hair is messy and my skin sticky, but I'm no Lauren. I don't have purple eyes, and I wasn't born with red hair that most women have to get in a box.

Nor would I ever be short with thin, toned legs and a flat belly and perfectly proportioned tits. I'm tall, I wear a size eight on a good month, and my breasts were never more prominent than a C, and that was when I breastfed for six months.

Lauren is perfect, that will never be me. I'm happy with that knowledge. She is a great girl and deserves to be perfect on the outside too.

Doesn't mean I don't get offers, I get a lot. Some guys like my curves. I have a great ass. I just haven't met a guy worth taking that step with.

Once bitten and twice shy is no made-up shit statement. Landon Bennet ruined me for other men. Not only was the guy gorgeous and successful, but he was a great lover.

I'm no fool to believe just any guy can give me that. I'm not going to waste my time.

Unfortunately, I know the biker in front of me wouldn't be wasting my time. By the way, he is peering at the beautiful Lauren. It's clear, I would've just wasted his.

No way would I ever hold a candle to Lauren. It's a sad day when a woman has to admit that she just got shit luck. I would've gone out with him, we both know it. And I would've opened my legs wider than he wanted it and just as quickly, and that too, we both know.

Too bad fate came to play and brought his true love.

I'm sure in the future they would have one great story to tell their kids. Who knows, maybe I'll still be around then.

My smile increases when the younger silent biker smacks River's head, snapping him out of his trance. I feel a longing and sadness that I just lost something important. But, I straighten my shoulders aware that I have been dismissed, and don't bother with goodbyes or pleasantries as I head on back to my humble abode.

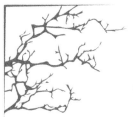

Chapter 4

When you run, you never realize you're doing it. You never think it's ever going to circle. You just presume you'd keep on running.

I stopped believing in God a long fucking time ago. I don't pray, I never hope.

The day I left Kanla I left my faith behind, abandoned my family and froze my heart. The only thing I took was my soul. I needed something to survive and I did.

Didn't ever think I'll come back and see Lauren standing on my front lawn.

Never thought I'll see her alone, unmarried, looking at me as if she still loved me, with a single tear sliding down her Ivory cheek.

She's still so fucking beautiful. Daisy Jane never told me Lauren still lived in my place, then again Daisy Jane never told me her friend Hannah had such a damn big mouth.

No wonder her man ditched her ass. She probably busted the guys' balls to smithereens.

I break my eye contact with Lauren as Killer smacks the back of my head, just in time to see Hannah walking to her house. Shit, I completely forgot about her. I flinch realizing that I just asked her out then basically got hooked on my past, forgetting her existence.

That must've stung, but it is what it is, Hannah is hot, but her mouth and her kids' temper tantrums aren't gonna make her memorable. Yeah, I'm a dick but it's the fucking truth.

So I shrug that off, and focus on the girl I actually came here for.

"You look good Lauren." Not sure why I say the obvious, still leaning on my bike.

She doesn't disappoint as she steps closer to the pavement, closer to me. That's Lauren for you, no matter how angry I got, how scary I looked, she never feared me.

"Daisy Jane told me you comin', I was just packing somethings to stay with Ms. Martha while you were in town." Her voice is so fucking uncertain, there is no anger there.

I fucking left her two days before our wedding. I didn't say goodbye. Where's the hitting, the swearing, shit, this is unreal.

I don't move as I stare into her purple gaze that I never got tired of. Her red hair practically fuckin' glows in the sun. I just stand there, again unable to even tell you if I'm breathing. So many memories.

Good memories, great. I'm here in front of our house, in the sun and I can't tell you why I left her.

Why the hell did I leave this woman?

I know I should tell her something, answer her question as she stands there in her tiny shorts looking like the young nineteen-year-old girl I left behind but I got no words. Never thought the day would come when I got nothing.

Killer nudges me and while most of the time I hate that

the fucking brother thinks it's okay to hit everyone when he fucking pleases I'm glad this time. Don't need to be acting pussy whipped when I got a missing woman to find.

Beggar comes first.

Lauren and me? I need to sort that shit out after. I can tell by her needy eyes that she wants us to be an us, and knowing Lauren she will forgive me when I say I'm sorry.

I plan to apologize, by then maybe I'll remember why I was so stupid to leave the one girl I've loved the most behind.

Right now I just can't remember why. She knew I belonged to The Satan Snipers, she accepted my rank in the government. Can't understand it, but I need to, for her sake more than mine.

So as much as I want to be selfish and say stay, I simply nod my head turn on my bike, swing my leg over it, twist the key that's already in the ignition and start my ride. Killer follows behind me and we mow town.

I don't go to the Clubhouse and Killer follows. I drive past, and fast on the open road and don't fucking stop. How the fuck did I leave her, why? Why can't I remember?

It's closing on seven when we make it back to the clubhouse, our gas close to empty. Thank Spade that the Kanla chapter decided to get their own gas tank or I won't be able to haul ass back to my place without riding bitch or taking a cage.

Killer and I didn't stop our bikes until we reached Barfa. I could tell my brother had a lot on his mind. Many thought he was completely emotionless but I know this Beggar chick meant something to him.

I see the way he worries, the extra hours he spends in the gym and it fucking kills me that the Kanla chapter think she's bad. My hands are tied by loyalty to National.

I can't say shit.

I can't even fucking tell them, Beggar is getting fucking tortured. Can't tell them I'm not just here to help them look for her, I'm here to make sure no one touches her once we found her.

Judging by Killers' attachment to Beggar I can see that even if I weren't around no one would harm the girl. I believe Killer will see to that.

The long ride and ten quiet minutes in Barfa, had been just what Killer and I needed. We made it back to the clubhouse just in time for supper. In all the chapters I've been to over the years they take mealtime very seriously. Which is a pleasing thing to me because I love food.

The cooking roster is a big thing in the club. Who we put on it is what makes it such a big deal.

It takes a huge amount of trust to allow someone to cook our food. So to be on the roster means that you are a full brother and our woman even if you're not fully patched in, it's still a big deal.

Our women take it very seriously. We don't call our females bitches like other motorcycle clubs. We always refer to them as 'woman'. They start off as kid, or dumb names while they earn their respect just like the brothers. But to be called 'woman' or by your club nickname is the highest honor.

The brothers don't all fuck the women, and the women aren't just here to look after us. They train like the brothers, some kill better than the brothers, like Mercy. They get important ranks just like the brothers, like our National road captain, After.

The only thing is we claim the women, some brothers, and our women prefer exclusivity and others prefer variety.

At the end of it all, we are just one huge fucking family. We eat together, sleep together. Some pray together and we fucking stay together until we die.

Kanla is lucky none of them have kids together 'cause in Denver, you can't take a piss without one little rugrat barging in. I never liked kids, don't know why but I just never take to them and trust me the feeling is mutual.

I can't believe that kid sat on my lap, can't believe Hannah named her kid Jo, no wonder she's crazy.

Killer doesn't wait for me or say a word once his Dyna is parked. I make my way up the porch steps and into the clubhouse following his retreating footsteps. The smell of disinfectant mingled with roast beef and fresh rolls instantly hit my nose and I don't waste time going to the dining room that is filled with my family.

I take my seat directly across Zero. The brothers and women nod heads and greet me as I walk to the other end. My chair scrapes and I notice the empty place of Kanla's Prez, Rounder.

I look to his daughter, Falon who is staring at Zero playing with his food with a frown on her face. Don't like how close she's sitting next to him. From what I know Zero has claimed Beggar.

Falon isn't part of The Satan Snipers, she's 'extended family' due to her relationship to the Prez, who isn't here.

"Where's your pops?" I ask her loud and clear.

"Sleeping, he wasn't feeling up for it today." She doesn't face me and I narrow my eyes at this information.

Since I've been here Storm has sat as President for every meeting. I think I've seen Rounder three times and all of those times the guy looked like fuckin' shit.

Cancer sucks fucking ass but a chapter is only as good as its President. And the Kanla Chapter's President can barely walk.

How the fuck is he supposed to run a Chapter of The Satan Snipers deadliest brothers? Because that's exactly what I have sitting around me.

These men that moved to start their own chapter in Kanla are the most sort out killers in the fucking world.

Killer alone has eight thousand confirmed kills. Spade is the best in close combat, while Knight is our long-distance shooter, he can make pretty damn any shot.

Zero is our all-round man, and best tracker we've got, he aces every fucking aspect of a perfect killer.

Too bad the fucker wants to waste it mooning over Beggar leaving him and not finding her. It'll make my job much simpler if Zero got off his fuckin' ass and helped but Prez's orders were to leave the brother alone.

So far, I've listened, but I'm starting to notice a lot of problems surrounding the club. Some of those problems are because of Beggar's leave.

The way she did it hurt some of them. They trusted her and they believe she betrayed them. If only they knew.

Another problem I noticed since my stay at the clubhouse is the strain from having a sick leader. None of the guys want to be the one to tell Rounder to step down, well none besides Killer, heard the brother told the man to hand in his patch.

He didn't listen.

Now he's always fuckin' sick leaving Storm to take his place.

These men aren't too happy to take orders from Storm, the boy is still a kid.

I look at all my brothers, aware that I can't particularly blame one of them for this mess because it's all of their faults. They are grown-ass men.

The one-woman patched in here, Venus has a sweet spot for Rounder. Clearly, they must have something akin to common sense.

They all know I'm aware of the situation happening around them, and that Storm the VP had to step up much sooner than National thought. I won't comment further.

I can feel eyes on me and I couldn't give a fuck. This is another problem I'm going to have to clean up.

The club is solid, all good brothers, but they're fucking blind to think that it's okay to keep Rounder as their Prez.

I'm not going to like informing National about this because not only is Storm, Rib's son but someone is going to have to step up and take Rounder's place and I'm dreading who it's going to be.

My eyes dart to Zero, the brother looks fucked. When Beggar left apparently the fucker smashed anything and everything he could find.

He even landed a punch to Killer. Worst mistake he made, Killer almost put him in the fucking hospital.

"Heard you getting shipped?" I ask Zero as my fork digs into the sliced beef casserole.

I lift the beef up and put it on my plate then proceed with dishing out veggies and still the brother doesn't answer.

Finally, I look up and instead of getting pissed I'm surprised to see him glaring at Falon who has since put her hand on his shoulder.

"What the fuck is your problem." He bellows, throwing his fork on the table.

Falon flinches, removing her hand from his body but it's much too late.

Shit just got real.

"I'm fuckin' talkin' to you Falon. I told you we done. I told you I claimed someone else but you still fuckin' touch me. So I'm going to tell you this one more time, so you get it in that thick head."

He looks at her with so much hatred that I kind of feel sorry for her but still you don't touch another woman's man when she's not here to see it.

"I don't want you to fuckin' touch me, I already claimed a woman and she sure as shit wasn't you, and wanna know what she did? She fuckin' betrayed me. I'm not making that fuckin mistake again, so stay the fuck away from me."

At that, I glance at the brother as he gets up, throws his chair back that it falls to the ground. We all sit here watching my brother march off.

Fuck, why did National put me here? I'm going to have to make a call, but before I do that I need some good fuckin' sleep.

Come tomorrow I'm going to be building a treehouse for Jo. So as much as I'd like to follow the brother, I eat my fucking food and don't ask anyone shit. The tension is thick in the air, everyone wants to leave the table besides Killer and Texas.

The two of them chat about football, loudly, eating more food, in no hurry to leave. And it's not for the first time I envy them for not having that emotion the rest of us have to live with.

It's almost nine when I start my bike. I don't twitch a muscle when Killer shows up mounting his Dyna.

"You want me to tell him?"

I don't look at the brother when he asks me that question, I rev my black beauty and shake my head in the negative. We ride the empty roads at full speed and don't stop until we park our bikes in front of my house.

From habit, my eyes track for suspicious people around us. The place is quiet and empty apart from the lone figure sitting on a step at Hannah's house. I know it's her and maybe someday I'll ask myself why I throw my keys at Killer and track on to her house but it's not today.

Today I sit directly opposite her and take the beer from her hand, today I drink from the same bottle she drank from and ask,

"Who names their daughter Jo?" I don't ask her for any other reason but to talk to her, not sure why because I really don't care why she named her kid Jo.

She chuckles,

"That'll be me. What are you doing this side of the fence River, couldn't get enough of my charm?."

I lift the beer up to my mouth, take a deep swallow and it goes down smooth. I glance at her dark form, the bridge of her nose, the fullness of her lips thinking of some many things I could say. Instead I just go for honesty,

"Fuck if I know, it just seemed like the thing to do."

"Yeah, it's peaceful isn't it."

I hear her rustle something and then hear the cap of a

beer getting popped before she lifts the bud to her mouth and swallows. We sit there on her steps in silence and it's fucking peace.

Not sure what time is it when she gets up off the step and stands up.

"Leaving so soon."

"We've been sitting here for two hours, I got church in the morning."

"Go out with me Hannah, one date." I can't explain why I'm insisting, why do I even think she'll say yes after my impromptu meeting with Lauren.

"Then what? I saw the way you looked at Lauren. I once looked at my ex-husband that way, I married him four months later. Don't waste your time on me River when she's waiting for you."

I'm not sure why her words get to me, but they do. I feel them deep in my soul,

"I left her right before our wedding, I'm not sure why, didn't think she still lived in my place. When I saw her today, I couldn't even talk to her."

Hannah's touch on my shoulder burns me up. Her fingers are long and firm as they rest on my shoulder,

"Lauren is a nice girl, and from what I heard since I moved here, Jake Stiles is an amazing guy. You don't know how lucky you are River to have someone wait for you."

"I never asked her to." Not sure why I feel the need to point it out.

"My mama used to say that everybody has a keeper, don't matter where life takes you, in the end, you'll know who's yours. My dad was hers, I thought I found mine when I married

Landon, but I realized mine came in a different form the day Jo was born, lord only knew why he brought me to Kanla, maybe it was to tell you this today, maybe not. Who knows what gods plans are right? Point I'm tryna make is, you need to know if Lauren is River's keeper, and it's not going to be while you on a meaningless date with your single parent neighbor."

I don't respond to any of what she says, instead, I keep my voice low,

"Goodnight Hannah."

Cold air takes the place of her fingers as she goes to the front door,

"Goodnight River."

I don't leave Hannah's porch steps even after her bedroom light goes off. I take in the fresh humid air, Hannah's words ringing in my ears. And it's only once I'm by my front door does her words finally hit, she said Rivers Keeper not Jakes.

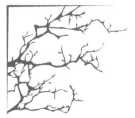

Chapter 5

There are many ways to spend a Sunday morning after church in Kanla. Lunch with family, breakfast at Ducky-Lows diner or a nice long swim at the public pool.

I would've done all of those today if Jo was around, but today is Tara's birthday. So, after church this morning I dropped her off at her six-year-old friend's place two blocks from our house.

Not sure what I was doing today except spending it with DJ. I was expecting her around ten. What I don't expect coming home as I park my Camry in the driveway is the two men I find at the back of my yard nailing planks to my tree.

I jump out of the car kicking the door with my three-inch heels. The sound of my hurried steps have both men turning around. The light grey knee-length pencil dress which is one of the few nice dresses I kept after my failed marriage rides up with my quick pace.

"Good morning Hannah." I recognize the younger biker from yesterday.

Today he's wearing a short-sleeve grey tee with his army tag hanging from the outside. His jeans are new and dark blue with a pair of very black sneakers.

What happened to using old clothes for building?

"Good morning to you too," I say cheerily, my hand going to shield my eyes.

"I didn't quite catch your name yesterday."

"That's because he didn't give it to you." At the sound of that unmistakable husky voice, I slant a glance to River who is standing near the tree with a two-meter plank in his grip.

My breath catches in my throat as a rush of warmth races over me. The memory of last night still fresh in my mind. He's dressed in a pair of very distressed denim and a black tee that stretches over his chest and arms.

His black boots have also seen better days but the get-up looks really attractive in an 'I don't give a shit way'.

"What happened Hannah Banana, you seem a little flustered there, finish pray for your sins?" I don't miss the sarcasm inked in his question or the way his light blue stare traces my body like a dog eyeing its treat.

I look good today. My expression says I know it, because I made an effort. I always do when I go to church.

"As a matter of fact I did, I also prayed for yours too." I try hard not to smile when he chuckles.

He doesn't say another word as he turns away from me and I admit I'm disappointed.

The young biker strolls right on overto were I'm standing. He extends his hand. It's the first time I get a good look at the guy.

"Names Killer."

He's absolutely fucking gorgeous. So gorgeous, I cream my panties staring into the bluest eyes I've ever seen in person.

His facial skin is smooth and shaven. My hand's envelope around his extended one feeling the power of his grip. The hardened calluses on his hand have me take another more in-depth glance into his gaze. And the blank coldness of his stare as he smiles tell me something about Killer - He isn't called Killer because of his looks.

I'm staring into the eyes of a killer. Seeing those tags around his neck, I don't feel danger. Quite opposite actually.

"Killer, I need help man." Killer winks at me as he releases the tight grip I have on his hand and saunters off.

It's passing eleven, DJ arrived a few minutes after I left the two men to their business. Well, not precisely left.

For the last thirty minutes, that's after I got lunch in the oven; DJ and I have been playing peeping tom through the bedroom window.

I watch River's naked back as he lifts a thick plank, and boy do I get an eye full. His muscles are ripped and covered in tattoos of various shapes, sizes, and colors. I've never had a guy so big before. It's not the first time I wonder what it'll be like to have a man like him under me, spreading me wide as I own him.

But that will never happen with River because this man has a beautiful woman who has already snatched his heart and will no sooner hold his body. That said body shines with a light sheen of sweat as he pulls on the rope that is used as a harness for the planks.

And Lord forgive me when I don't stop admiring all the

planes of his back and arms. Even knowing he isn't mine and will never ever be mine, I salivate at just the wonder of it.

Isn't that what single parents do? We feast from afar that which we can never have.

The tap on my shoulder and ice-cold bottle on my neck startle me. I jump with a scream.

"I swear to fuckin' Christ I'm going to kick your ass woman," I curse, grabbing the beer from her outstretched hand.

Taking a long sip from her own bottle, DJ's green steady focus observes me with a contemplative gleam in them.

"So you don't want a drink then?"

My answer is to plant my ass on the bed, take a long swig of my bud. Her red painted on lips thin before she throws her head back in a good old fashion DJ laugh.

"Oh, my fuckin' word Nay you should see your face."

She smirks. That devil smile of hers never gets old. The all-knowing glance she gives me right before she saunters up next to me on the bed tells me that my red and white-haired best friend knows exactly what I want but could never have.

Even DJ knows I don't stand an inkling of a chance apart from a single night with River right?

River will give me that, I'm certain.

The question is - Will I be able to live with that?

What if he and Lauren remain my neighbors? I know I just met the guy but there is something so warm about him. Akin to a home that is a person.

I can't explain it.

He just feels like a guy you instantly melt into. A person that once you meet them it's just as sudden as you are familiar with them.

Maybe it's because DJ is his first cousin. But I doubt it's the reason he has me all twisted up.

Too bad the first guy I crush on since Landon happens to be the famous Jake Stiles, the town's hero.

DJ informed me earlier that it was River who sent The Satan Snipers to Kanla. Now here he is building my kid a treehouse.

I stop spying after I finish off my drink and head on off to the kitchen to take the chicken out of the oven.

The roast potatos and rolls have since cooled down so I go about setting the table outback.

DJ arrives outside with a few cold drinks and four cups in her hands.

"Where's the inner slut, Nay?" She whispers as she glances up at the two men.

"Go there and tell him you would love to go out with him. You'd never know, he might love the sex kitten. I mean he probably fucks the women in his club. Surely he admires an exhibitionist in the bedroom."

I blatantly ignore the last part of her statement and focus on the second,

"You think?" I ask.

I let her in on everything regarding her cousin, including last nights encounter, the moment she arrived. There wasn't much I left out because I hardly spoke to him.

DJ is my coke to my jack. I am talking to the woman who is the only family I have besides Jo. DJ and I have been inseparable since we got together years ago.

I wiped her vomit from my floor when she went on her benders, never did I judge her.

She taught Jo how to count to a hundred while she babysat for me without asking for a dime, and not one day did she ever complain.

Last year my kid had gastrointestinal problems. I couldn't afford the nanny every day and taking a day off wasn't even an option.

DJ was the only one I could really count on.

Not mentioning the numerous times she turned my worst days into happy ones with her craziness. Or the millions of days the two of us just got down on the floor and started talking 'til the sun came up.

We both step into the kitchen and hoping also out of earshot.

"Yes. You should've seen the way he was looking at your ass now. If you think he at least doesn't want a little piece then you should not be doing medicine, clearly, you failed chemistry."

My lips tug at the mention of my studying. Way to boost a woman's ego.

"But there's Lauren."

She rolls her eyes in exasperation,

"Lauren is beautiful and sweet, and not for River. He left her once, maybe he was just shocked when he saw her yesterday."

She shrugs, gliding her fingers through her long hair,

"You got nothing to lose, you act as if you contemplating a crime when really it's a night of getting laid."

I groan, looking up to the white ceiling.

"I swear I'm so going to regret this."

"Good regrets Nay." She pats my back as her denim covered long legs take her outside.

Leaving me to my decent sized open plan kitchen. It's not the first time I think 'fuck I love my friend.'

Grimacing, I stare hard at the yellow and red flower wallpaper.

I need to paint this house. Unfortunately, that can't happen anytime soon.

A strong reminder that not only am I always just getting by but I don't really have anything to offer in a relationship.

I got no love besides for my kid, no money, a used up body and a new mortgage.

The sound of a car driving up my driveway has me checking out the window as my stomach does a flip.

I huff in frustration seeing Gregory Deane step outside his car and walk toward my back yard to shake River's hand. Rushing around the kitchen, I fetch the roasted chicken from the cooling rack, holding it with oven mitts.

I don't like the fact that Gregory is here. Not sure why he assumes that he can just pop on over whenever the mood strikes. I put up with it for two reasons- One he is the deputy and two I got no man to watch over Jo and me. Plus he isn't a douche like the sheriff.

"Oh No."

I hear the tone of DJ's voice and quickly jump back from the kitchen window. I feel like a teenager only this time I actually am hormonal.

I follow DJ's voice outside, taking a moment to enjoy the view of River's ripped form.

He turns and stares at me. And the look he gives me melts the red thong I put on this morning.

"And there she is, I was beginning to wonder when miss peeping tom would show herself." I stand gob smacked.

My cheeks burn with the embarrassment of getting caught. It's a moment in my life where I can't hide my shameful truth because it's slapped across my face and decorated in red.

The Deputy greets me as I slant a glance to River who is watching Gregory eye-fuck my body.

River casually walks right up to me, his sweaty arm going around my hip. And fuck me not, I am officially turned on and too stunned to say a thing.

"Deputy." River's deep voice emanates through the air.

"Jake. It's been a while."

"What brings you to Hannah's place." River obviously not one to beat around asks him straight out. But he keeps his voice cool as his fingers grip my hip showing me something else, something confusing.

It shows me that maybe this biker who makes me feel things I thought I would never feel again could have a deeper interest in me besides the ride he wishes to take my body on.

I am woman enough to admit that I get a sick satisfaction out of it.

A woman can always dream right? Maybe, DJ is right, after all, maybe I can charm the biker with my sexual moves.

If there is one thing, I'm sure of, it's that I'm great in bed. Which brings the reason as to why I had such a hard time when Landon screwed me over.

At least with River, I'll know exactly what I'm getting. A one night stand of hot sex with a big bad biker.

There will be no follow-ups or sweet-talking, besides the moans he fucks out of me.

Hand holding and skin touching would be limited to my nails digging into his back, and his hands gripping my ass.

At least this time I'm aware of what it is - A meaningless night of wild sex.

For me, it'll be a night to remember. For River, I'd be just another fuck until he locked his keeper.

I hope by the end of it I'm still standing.

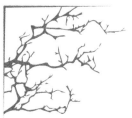

Chapter 6

There aren't many moments in my life when I can say I wasn't thinking or didn't really have a choice.

Today as I stand with Hannah wrapped in my arms while my fingers dig into her hips, I can honestly say that I'm fucking thinking, only I'm doing it with my dick.

And when dicks are involved and a woman like Hannah is up for the taking there's a whole fuck load of balls getting weighed with it. The only problem is Deputy Fuckwad Gregory, looking a little too closely at what I already won.

We both know who has the bigger balls.

"Just came to pop in and check if everything's fine." His words are meant for me but his eager brown eyes are still glued on Hannah.

Killer's silent feet moves behind me, but close enough that I can sense the ghost's presence. No doubt he is sizing the beige deputy outfit this dick is wearing.

"I'm fuckin' hungry," Killer declares, "drop the balls contest brother, let's go eat, and whoever the fuck you are get lost it's clear the woman has already chosen."

Killer walks off after he says his piece going straight for the food.

"That's enough!." Hannah screams as she wriggles her body wanting to leave my arms but this isn't my first rodeo. I easily maneuver her with the same hand I'm using to hold her form until her ass is right in front of my dick and my arms securely locked around her.

Of course, she-devil digs her fingers into my arm that's wrapped tightly around her torso.

But I got to hand it to Hannah, the woman is classy.

I expect her to throw a fit, or do some wild thing but she merely cinches my skin with her nails, that feel like small pokey weapons.

She sighs and smiles at the Deputy who I forgot is even here,

"Deputy, didn't expect to see you so soon. Is there a problem?"

Deane's nostrils flare and I don't miss the subtle tell he gives Hannah which just pisses me right the fuck off.

"What the fuck is going on, just spill it!." I glower at him as I say this, waiting to hear the real reason this fucker decided to pop on in.

He clenches his jaw but I can hear his fucking beating heart race at a hundred miles a minute all the way over here.

"We found two dead bodies yesterday, just a couple miles out of town..."

"What that gotta do with Hannah?" I interrupt him, not liking a bit of where this conversation is heading.

He finally addresses me,

"They were women, both badly beaten to death. Nadine Harper's kids found the bodies early hours of this morning. Just wanted to give a heads up, Hannah needs to be aware of this because it's the same road she frequents on a Wednesday."

"She's aware, now leave," I tell him in my deadliest voice as the little she witch goes another round pinching my arms.

"What River meant to say was that I'm glad you stopped by and thanks for the warning," Hannah informs the dick, going completely off course to what I just said.

Good thing I do repeats.

"No, I said what I meant to say the first time. Leave."

The sheriff takes one long look at Hannah before he shakes his head and saunters off toward his crappy car.

I release Hannah from my stronghold only after he's gone. She spins instantly around, her curly hair fanning out, her grey eyes glaring at me and fuck it this chick is sexy.

"You had no business acting like that River." She yells as her hands fly in the air, "It was rude and completely out of character. I do not appreciate you comin' here and acting as if you own me while pining for another."

I frown as I take a step closer, "What did you just say?"

Her big half-circle shaped eyes become full moons at the tone of my voice and the entreat of my steps, "Own you? Baby I haven't even begun to thaw you out, but tonight I'm going to fucking own your body Hannah and it's going to be one hell of a fuckin' claiming ."

Her mouth gaps open, she's practically fuming while my dick is pulsing. Something passes her eyes before she pulls a three-sixty and sighs instead, jutting out her hip,

"Yes, tonight you will own me, for now, let's just eat." I watch the little she-witch swing her hips from side to side and I swear if my dick can sing it'll be on full blast.

HANNAH

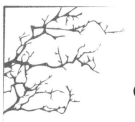

Chapter 7

What is life with no regret, what is a beaten soul without remorse? What defines you better than experience? Isn't that what it is all about. The rights and wrong that make us, the scars that riddle our end with memories that shape us into who we are. I watched him for longer than I should.

I contemplated on ways on how it will go as I sat across the man who made me feel. I never knew a man like River.

The more I watched him, the deeper I fell into the pitfall of his gaze seeing a mirror of myself, a reflection of a human scorned. It was on that Sunday at the back of my yard that I finally saw the torture in his gaze.

DJ spoke and I answered but my eyes never wavered from the man that would have my body by the end of the night. This man, that would ultimately ruin me in one breath. The daylight ended its heated mess when Killer and DJ left and still I watched him.

I'm on the step of my porch, my body heated with thoughts of this man. He picks up the rest of the tools and puts it on the top of the wood that's stacked up into two rows. He turns to me, his eyes that of a cold man. His body a weapon.

I watch him as I know him but I don't really see him. This isn't how I thought it will go.

He walks up to me and my knees buckle at the awareness of his gaze. River doesn't utter a word as he grips my butt cheeks.

Instinct has me locking my legs around his hips. My chest beats with hard thuds as I lift my eyes to his brooding dark stare.

His lips lock on mine and my body goes into limbo. Stars burst behind my closed eyelids as his tongue takes ownership of my mouth.

My body convulses when his fingers dig into my ass cheeks. His grip is solid and consuming me.

My back hits the door.

I feel the door part but I don't stop kissing this man. He is eager in his claiming. I wouldn't be able to tell whether his heart accelerated because it's all happening so fast. I am spinning, my head deep under the spell of this biker, who is kissing me as if I am the air he breathes while he floats in space.

My body rubs against his and just before I lose my mind, he sweeps aside my g-string.

I faintly hear River's zip slide down and before I know it the head of his cock is lining my entrance. I was wet earlier but now I'm drenched. He never talks, he seeks no permission as he enters my body and I kill you not I scream fucking pain before the tip of his cock even hits deep into me that I convulse in instant pleasure.

"Fuck. I'm not gonna fit fully in." He grunts in a mixture of smugness and irritation.

I look down in a daze at his length and girth.

He is thicker than Landon but not longer. So I do what any hot horny thirty-year-old woman would, I tell him,

"Push it in it will fit."

He looks like he wants to refuse but I am a very sexual woman so I tilt my hips and make a melting sound.

And it works way too well when he pushes my back hard against the wall that my mouth parts open.

He wastes no time guiding his cock to my entrance. River pushes in so forcefully, my walls stretch and tear. I feel an immense amount of pleasure and even more pain. So I scream. It's loud and he makes a move to pull out but my legs lock around his ass, and I order,

"Fuck me."

River kisses me when the words leave my mouth, not a slow kiss, but one I would remember as shattering.

His tongue tangles with mine sucking on my own until it's painful and then, only then he starts fucking me.

He pulls his cock out until the tip is stuck in the front of my walls and lunges in hard, deep and so fucking thorough. Gyrating his hips. I hiss and claw at his back until I'm scraping skin.

His skin gets sweaty and I have nothing to hold me to him so I grip his hair and meet him thrust for thrust. And it's then that River claims me and what ownership it is.

With every push and every pull, he takes me until I'm

screaming in bliss. I'm screaming in pleasure and he doesn't stop. Not when I pull on his neck, suck on his skin.

My ass in his hands, my cunt gripping onto his dick and still he fucks me. I bite him, I scrape at his drenched salty skin and still, he fucks me deep and hard.

I want to hold off.

I want to breathe and not succumb to this addiction that has taken over my senses but I can't.

My body pulls taught, my womb contracts and I'm coming.

They say when you fly too high that gravity always wins. I reach beyond gravity, and I don't stop until I'm floating.

River doesn't grunt, he doesn't let himself go, there is no explosion like my own. I open my eyes and like every other time in my life reality stumbles.

I watch him, as I know him but I don't really see him. His eyes are that of a cold man. His body a weapon.

And when he entered my body, I inhaled easier. When he touched me I breathed all that was him and then he took me, opened me up and with each thrust I felt new.

I felt free.

For that time 'till night broke away the day, I was his but he wasn't mine yet. He was his own. His cold eyes lock on mine and in it is glimpses of epic splendor.

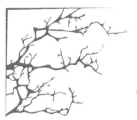

Chapter 8

My mind jumbles as my dick remains hard. I've learned many years ago that I can't do it. I can't come unless a woman is utterly helpless.

As I stand here now with Hannah convulsing in the after-effects of what my dick has given many women before and her doughy eyes on my own, I am the one helpless.

I want to fuck her cunt, I need to take her ass as I rope her body into a statue of my making, only then will I come. Only then will I make her mine but I can't.

Hannah is too innocent, she's too needy. I thought I could do it. I convinced myself that I could fuck her without feeling a thing of remorse besides my dick needing a good work out.

But thinking and doing are two utterly opposite words. I should've known of better.

Hannah doesn't need a man ruining her any more than she already is. I slowly put her down knowing our time has come to a stop.

She is forgettable. I will forget this and move on as I have many times before and will do many more times in the future.

"What? That's it."

I drop my eyes to the floor at the sound of her incredulous voice.

"Yeah, that's it."

I shrug my shoulders feigning my 'I don't give a fuck' face and tuck my hard dick into my jeans.

The sound of my zipper going up is heard way too fucking loud.

Hannah says not a thing more as she stands there with her hands crossed under her breast. Her dress is askew and she makes no attempt to straighten it.

I don't dare look into her eyes.

Not to say I'm a coward, it's just to show her that I don't give a shit.

Which, I don't, she's forgettable it would be easy to stay away.

I turn around, walk toward the door, not realizing what I'm leaving behind when I open that door.

I wish I can see my future.

I wish I could know now that soon I would wish I turned around.

I would wish that I spent those extra hours with her.

But at this point, I know nothing besides that I got to get to the clubhouse.

People always say time is free because it never stops, never ends.

An ongoing cycle of life until death.

How could we truly be free though? When our life is measured by years lived, money earned, knowledge gained, power of forgiveness, worship, and prayer. It is filled with challenges. Filled with moments we don't always choose, memories we want to forget.

All of that happens and still, time passes. So are we really free? Because the only time I feel close to free is when I'm on my bike. And even then I am not truly free because death is there waiting patiently for me to make a wrong move.

I glide through Kanla streets and leave another past behind me. Me and my bike riding as one.

When I hit the long empty road, I rev up my engine speed and I let go of my worries as I just focus on the road.

I have no destination in mind as my body moves to the ballad of my bike.

Most of my club brothers refer to their bikes as a living person, some call it he or she, others name them.

I have never looked at my own motorbike as a living thing. My motorbike has always been a machine that gives me a piece of freedom.

A thing which allows me to hold my life in my own hands for that short time as I power it up with every bend, every curve, moving carelessly through the people trapped in their cages. My bike promises me that when I sit on it I will falsely believe that my time is free.

I move far, I go fast, and I don't stop until I reach the Kanla clubhouse.

Knight and Texas sit on the steps nursing a beer bringing back an unwanted memory of Hannah and I doing the exact same thing just yesterday. I pull my helmet off and untie my bandana from around my mouth.

"Didn't think I'd be seen you so soon, what happened to the hot momma you were banging?." Knight yells.

I shake my head as I move closer to the two brothers who are both wearing their cuts.

Can't say I'm in the least bit surprised Killer told the club. He never sees the need to lie or shut the fuck up.

"Are you gonna pass me one of those or are you gonna sit there wondering if my balls are still heavy?" I say to the brother.

Knight throws his head back in a roaring laugh while Texas passes me a court.

I snap it open and tip it back taking a deep swallow. I move between them heading for the door.

"Might wanna sit your ass right over here, ain't wanna go in there now." Texas's warning stops me mid-step.

The man isn't known for a lot of words. My back still to both of them.

My beer in my right-hand dangling from my fingers.

I ask, "What's going on?"

"We called votes today, Rounder's out, you in and Storm is gone trigger fuckin' happy, as I said you ain't wanna go in there. Sit your ass over here," Texas informs me and I swear to fucking Christ that I am hearing this shit wrong. Me, in? Fuck.

I don't turn to the partially drunk brothers instead I take the two steps to the door and open it just as the sound of a silencer and a glass-shattering ring through my ears.

I've always considered myself a calm man. Someone who could solve a problem without the bloodshed or hurt others would cause.

But I kill you fucking not that my blood pressure fucking rises at the sight of this place. A half-dressed Storm sits on the three-piece sofa that just yesterday looked like brand spanking new, now the couch is fucked. Ripped with deep knife holes and white pieces sticking out.

My eyes slowly take in the area. It's a fucking mess. Shattered glass surfaces the entire floor. Every place my eyes follow is destroyed. There are bullet holes in the wall and it's then I fucking lose it.

"What. The. Fuck?" My voice booms through the air and the Vice President doesn't even move an inch.

"If it isn't the new Prezi Prezi Prezi." He slurs, naked back hunched into a deep arch.

From narrowed eyes, I glare at his slouched form looking so defeated on the couch.

"Well thank fuck they didn't vote you in brother. Where's the fuckin' respect? This is the Clubhouse you swore to fuckin' protect, look at this place, it looks like a dump."

He chuckles as he lifts his head to face my standing form,

"Already making orders now are we."

"If I was, it will be throwing your fuckin' ass out."

Storm jumps up from the couch but it's sloppy, "No need to kick me out, I'm fucking gone."

"You drunk, sleep it off, I'm not letting you leave in this state."

He takes a drunken step toward me and I cross my arms over my chest and arch a brow.

I have no qualms about beating a drunk brother.

How many of them did it to me when I fucked up.

"Who died and made you my boss." He spits on the floor after he's done talking.

"Apparently Rounder is dying and now I am your fucking President whether I want to be or fuckin' not. So, stop the bitching a grow a pair of balls, sleep it off. We got church in the morning and you of all people want to be there." I say my piece then I march around the corner and up the stairs to the rooms.

My mind is too tired to think now. My body too fucking wired up to take anymore of anybody's shit tonight.

I'm reaching for Knight's room when I spot Venus leave

her own. One look at the hot long-haired woman and my dick pulses. Venus knows how I like it. She understands how I need it so I push the tinge of guilt that hits me, the speck of reason that assaults my mind, telling me I'm doing something wrong and I walk up to her.

I grab her hair in a tight grip.

My mouth hovering over hers,

"You know what I want, are you gonna give it to me?"

Her tongue darts out touching my lips. All the answers that I need and want are in that action. And I know by morning I will be satiated.

My dick will be rung dry and balls a hell of a lot lighter. I wish I knew the regret I'd feel once it was all over.

HANNAH

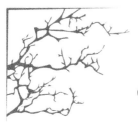

Chapter 9

"Cadence asked if I'm going to the fair this weekend. I said I'd ask. Can I go momma?."

Jo got her hands on either side of the red plastic trolley, her feet are balanced at the bottom while I push her around and do the shopping. Most of the kids in Kanla do it so I don't stop her.

After work today I picked Jo up and brought her to the shopping center not far from the hospital where I work. It's a Friday afternoon and payday, so the place is packed.

This weekend is the Barbeque weekend, for the entire town. Some do theirs at home but most folks in Kanla prefer to go to the kid's fair. There is live music from local bands, kids rides and lots of stalls but also a ten-dollar entrance fee. Something which I just don't have to spare at the moment.

I haven't had the heart to tell my kid no as yet, more so now when she is looking at me with those eager grey eyes of hers.

"We'll see Jo, let's get this shopping done and head on home, then maybe later we can talk about the fair while we eat ice-cream." I smile as her face breaks into a huge grin, damn my kid is pretty.

It's not the last time that I think to myself that I did well. Really good.

I make a zooming sound and pretend I'm running while I push the trolley with Jo still on for the ride. I turn the corner and my movements instantly stop at the sight before me.

My momma once told me that sometimes a past needs to stay where it is. And other times you pretend it's still in the past when it's somewhere dangling in the future just waiting to sneak up on you. Somehow you just avoid facing it, you deny that it is still very much there in your present too.

As I stand here on the corner of the sixth aisle in the grocery store I see a past that happened a little over three months ago because I have avoided it in all aspects of the word. It is now my mother's words ring true again.

Over three long months have gone since my brief encounter with him. He tainted me in one weak moment when I succumbed to my needy flesh. When I gave in to the pull I felt toward this man. Then he ripped it away without a backward glance.

It was that night that I found my story behind the man named River because that night he didn't just shatter me, he made me bath in a river of regret until I drowned.

I'm sure it's a couple of seconds that pass by even though it feels like forever as I stare into his cold blue gaze.

Lauren stands next to him with a basket in her hand also still, quiet. She looks breathtaking in the long floral dress and her red hair falling down her back. River stands next to her with his distressed jeans, white Henley and imposing form, forever the protector.

The ripple of hurt suffocates me yet I bid it stay inside. I urge myself to accept reality for what it is, reality is truth. They look meant to be.

They are meant to be.

I was just a passing to this man. *The woman who couldn't even make him come.*

I turn my vision to the Italian biker and two female bikers

watching them as they each push a trolley down the baking section oblivious to the tension in the air.

Jo turns her head and spots River. She jumps off the trolley way too quickly and rushes off to River throwing herself into him.

Unfortunately, while I avoided River, Jo felt no need to do the same. She spots his bike in his driveway on odd occasions and rushes off to talk to him. He has been taking her out the past two months.

I never question it, and he never minds so there is nothing more to say.

I have accepted that my kid and him are close. I also accepted that he will never be mine.

I push my trolley forward ready to be done with this before my emotions bleed through my eyes.

Before River, my life seemed like it was going in the direction I wanted it too.

After a brief encounter with the man, I thought it all through and took a step back and what I saw was a lost woman who learned how to survive in the middle of the ocean with all the dangers lurking around.

I saw a woman who though lived to see another day would never learn to swim to shore.

A light whistle snaps me out of my dark reverie and I look up into brown small eyes attached to rich olive skin.

The Italian biker smiles a sexy smile,

"Yo mama. You are one fine looking woman."

My brows arch seeing this charming man standing so tall right next to me. His steady gaze alert yet playful.

And I can't help the words that leave my mouth, "A

fine-looking woman like me and a sexy guy like yourself will make one hell of a night."

The small smirk on my face is my giveaway that I'm joking but the heat in his eyes that turn smoldering before my own tells me he ain't.

He licks his lips,

"Who says we got to make it just a night when I can easily make it a month." My eyebrows shoot up and before I can even reply he wraps his fingers around my hand I have on the trolley,

"Names Knight, want to go out on a date?"

My mind instantly goes back to River when he asked me out and the churn in my gut makes me sober. I'm about to refuse when familiar hands wrap around my waist, pulling me closer to a chest I have only been close to twice. Once in this very same position.

"She's taken." Those two words hit me like a bucket of cold water and a bag of ice. Knight looks to me then to River before he nods and saunters off.

I wriggle out of his grip as Mrs. Cary turns into the aisle, the woman takes one look at the bikers and a glimpse at me before she turns her trolley around.

I spin around and poke the asshole in his chest.

"Who the hell do you think you are, coming and laying claim to me like I'm one of your whores. You had your chance you weren't man enough to take it now it's over."

I make a move to push him when he grips my arm, his angry eyes seeping into mine,

"I gave you three months to get over your shit Hannah. If you good to flirt with another man then you fucking good to be with me."

He leaves me thereafter, with my kid's hand in his and I just stand there thinking 'what the fuck'.

I don't have to question the safety of my kid, I know River will keep her safe.

I don't understand what just happened. I don't get where he is going with this. I thought he moved on, I thought he found his keeper in Lauren. I never thought the biker wanted me.

I try to think if I missed something, if maybe I wasn't looking closely enough but all I can see is the hurt he left in me. All I can feel is the pain that he didn't see that day when turned his back on me.

I'm not sure how I make it home. I'm not sure when I even get here. I just know that River will be back with my daughter soon.

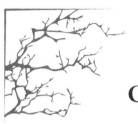

Chapter 10

In my world rank is earned by respect. You don't just wake up one morning and decide this is where you are going to be placed. You got to bleed for your brothers, you got to put it all on the line for us knowing without a doubt that we got your back.

You got to understand that we are your family by choice. That when the world chooses everyone else we will always choose you.

It has been a long road these past thirteen weeks since the night I was given the title of President for the Kanla chapter of The Satan Snipers.

Storm has been my biggest challenge since becoming President but even he has come around.

There has been an enemy in our midst. People in Kanla, women especially are getting murdered right under our noses.

The Satan Snipers have vowed to protect this town and we will.

But today isn't that day. Today I'm spending time with Jo, at the back of the Clubhouse by the lake.

She's licking her chocolate flavored ice-cream, double scoop or nothing my girl always says. Yes, she is my girl, my kid now.

My relationship with Jo is something special. She is the only piece of Hannah I got.

While it isn't the piece I wanted, it's pretty fucking special.

Since my night with Hannah, I have lived with regret.

Why? I can't fucking say.

Since then I have tried talking to her but she runs the other way. I knew I hurt her that day but fuck since my night with Venus my balls are blue.

I haven't taken another woman in my bed since the morning I woke up with Venus naked next to me. After that, it was like an obsession for Hannah grew. I spent weeks spying on her until I had to buckle up and finally be the President.

Finding Beggar and the club has been my priority since then and when I'm not doing that I have been spending time with Jo and boy is the kid a talker.

"The fare is tomorrow, can we go?" Jo asks me and I mentally check my plans for tomorrow.

"Yeah, sure, why not." I pull the end of her hair as she sucks on a small blob of ice cream that fell on to her hand.

"Can we take momma with us too?" She looks up at me with a goofy smile on her chocolate smothered face. That shit is all over her face and teeth.

"Yeah, your momma is definitely coming tomorrow."

I don't inform her that her mother will be coming in

another way too. I just stare out toward the lake. At peace just to have the kid next to me and my brother's at the back.

There is only one thing missing now. Well, two if you think about Beggar.

The other is a grey-eyed feisty woman that I haven't really gotten to know besides a glimpse of what she was, is.

But that was all I needed to become this man who is obsessed with her. The man who wants to kill every mother fucker for just looking at her.

The sun begins to set when Jo and I make it back to her house. Hannah as always is sitting on the stairs, a bud light in her hand.

She has since changed into tight fitted jeans and a blue tee that does wonders for her tits. Hannah spots us jumping out of the truck I borrowed from Texas and gets up walking toward us. Jo rushes off the minute I open the door and meets Hannah halfway, giving her an ear full.

I watch the two of them for a minute. Both animated in their storytelling. They are so much alike it's shocking. Her kid took after her mother which meant the father was a puss.

He better never step foot in my territory because I will end him. These are mine now. I just got to convince Hannah.

They both turn toward the house when Hannah stops and flings her head around to face me, "Aren't you coming?"

I give her a chin dip, "Just enjoying the view for a bit."

She rolls her eyes as Jo giggles and walks into the house. After a minute I look around the area for anything suspicious and also signal Spade, who has been watching Hannah's place from my spare bedroom for weeks.

Once everything is clear I head on inside Hannah's place.

Remembering my manners, I look around the house, to say something nice, but there is nothing.

It's falling apart.

The skirting boards are almost out. The walls are fucked and going to have to be plastered. There is no use fixing it up.

Why the fuck would she buy such a crappy place? I don't say that though because I know just as fast as I was invited, I would be out. So I bite my fucking tongue and follow Jo's voice.

"...to the fair momma."

"Jo I'm sure River has a lot of better things to do than go to a fair," Hannah informs Jo who is sitting on the yellow kitchen counter that is as old as my great grandmother.

"No, I don't," I say on entry with a big smile painting my lips.

Hannah glares at me and if looks could kill.

Fuck

"This is between me and Jo, butt out of it."

"Momma that's rude," Jo says.

"Just tell her." I chuckle when Hannah gives me another one of her death glares.

"Jo, go and wash up so you can eat. River and momma need to have a conversation."

Jo jumps down and rushes off. I lean against the wall, cross my arms over my chest, and place one foot in front of the other.

"I'm waiting," I say this because if there is one thing I've learned about Hannah is the woman got attitude.

"So, you not with Lauren?"

My eyes shoot up at the question. I didn't see that one coming. Then It hits me, why she would think that.

"Why don't you kiss me first and then ask me that again."

"Kiss you, I haven't seen you River, you had a chance and you didn't even want to take it. Now I know you and Jo are close and I can respect that but you and I are never happening again."

Her voice is so calm as she says those words that it is like she has accepted it. I don't like it, not one bit.

People don't accept things without regret, need, longing.

People don't just decide that they are going to take one path without at least testing another. I look into her eyes and I'm blinded by the hurt in them.

"I'm not with Lauren, she was for Jake. I left that life a long time ago. I became River, a man that needs a keeper. And Lauren ain't it Hannah, now I found my keeper in a little girl. Names Jo, and I'm pretty sure it's a package deal. I ain't saying we going to work woman but at least give me a fucking chance."

She stares long and hard, and I stare back. I ain't going to hide shit from her now. I need her to see that I want this.

It takes forever before she sighs.

"One date, and that's the fair. You screw it up and I'm done River."

I smile and stand up straight,

"Yes ma'am."

"And go wash up for dinner."

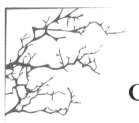

Chapter 11

I woke up this morning and went straight to my mirror. I asked myself is this who I am. Was I seriously giving River, the man who walked away without even a snicker of regret another chance? I was.

Because even though he hurt me. He has been good for Jo. She smiles a lot when he brings her back.

The sound of my phoning ringing has me rushing to where I left it charging. I hit the coffee table with my knee and curse, not even looking at the screen I pick it up,

"Hello."

"Morning Hannah banana."

I squeak, "Hi." *How the hell did he get my number?*

"I'm on my way you got an hour woman." River cuts the call before I even reply. I stare at the phone and my mind is still processing that twenty-two-second call.

It's almost an hour that passes, I'm just putting my purple pumps on when the knock sounds on the door. Jo rushes right past me and throws the old thing open. I stand up to my full height and my mouth waters at the vision before me.

He's wearing a new pair of black jeans, a white and red pair of Jordan's with a black tee under his cut, that now has the title of President on the left side of his jacket. Which means he is now the President of the club.

I'm not surprised by this because DJ has kept me on the 'I need to know' regarding River. And that 'need to know' was everything.

"Hey River," Jo practically yells.

"Morning kid." He pulls her hair as he comes through the door and my stomach makes a funny noise just before he walks on up to me and kisses me smack on the lips.

The leer in his gaze makes me flush and I bite my lip.

"Morning Hannah."

I mumble a response and practically run to the door where my five-year-old stands giggling. I leave the keys in the door already knowing River will lock up.

It's twenty minutes later when we leave the air-conditioned truck and step on out into the chaos of the town's annual fair.

Jo holds my hand as River keeps his pace a foot behind us. I don't question this because like all the folks in town, I know about the recent deaths in Kanla. We also know The Satan Snipers are trying to catch the killers.

Jo tugs on my hand as River pays our entrance fee. I bend my back, dropping my ear.

"All the Satan Snipers are here momma, look."

I lift my head and as true to form it is basically all of them.

A touch on my lower back gets me standing upright. I spin

around ready to give someone either a hug or a punch when I see it's only River.

"Did you know that your entire club is going to be here?" Is what comes out.

"Yup." He pops out the p.

"Is it because of all those murders?"

"Something like that." His eyes steal the rest of my questions with a promise of later.

His hand interlocks mine with a stolen comfort of more. It's in those two actions that I know River is here for me. He is giving himself to me. Offering me him.

Jo moves to the other side of River and we head straight for the Ferris wheel. It is a long line to stand in and the Southern sun is making the wait even longer.

"You ever been on this thing before?" I ask River who still got his hand in mine.

"Yeah, fifteen years ago I spent the entire day on this wheel. DJ insisted I bring her here, wasn't good for my reputation to be seen taking my cousin so I saw the Ferris wheel and said fuck it. I don't think Daisy Jane has been back since." He squeezes my hand as my face stretches into a big smile.

"That explains a lot. Every year I ask her to join but she always has an excuse."

"That's Daisy Jane, she's a once bitten never chance it kinda girl."

Our turn comes an hour later. I'm sticky and sweaty in my denim shorts and spaghetti strap top. River is wearing way more than me and he hasn't broken out a sweat. He hasn't complained. We've been talking about DJ then his club and finally Jo and him. I knew they had gotten close but not so close, I am actually a tinge bit jealous.

Especially now, because the ride only has place for two people on one seat. And my kid insists on sitting next to River, not me.

I end up sitting next to Mr. Crane and the old fart stinks like old beer mixed with sour cream, yuck. And every time the breeze blows I taste it in my mouth.

My head begins to spin with an underlying headache while my kid and River laugh and put their hands up having the time of their lives.

I'm going to kick his butt the minute I am done here. I swear, vow to myself for the full seven minutes of the ride that I am going to kill River ten times over.

By the time the ride is done, the inside of my head resembles the inside of a rock concert.

My temper is fire and my determination short-lived when he carries Jo down then turns to me beaming.

I have never seen the man look so young, carefree. It's something else and knocks me of quilter.

"That was good." And just those words leaving his lips simmers my anger.

I guess a headache isn't so bad.

I give my kid a hug, "You liked it?"

"Best ride ever, River said we can go again later."

I am not going on that ride later, I don't say that to either of the two happy go lucky campers.

I just smile and scratch the top of my kid's head.

Four hours later and seven rides under my day belt I'm

finally done. I never liked rides, and right now that isn't changing anytime soon.

After a long tiring day, we are finally heading home. We are in the truck, Jo is sleeping.

"I take it you didn't have a good time?" River says this to me as my eyes remain cast on the dry country road.

"It was okay, I guess. I'm not a fan of fair rides. Never liked it."

He chuckles at my confession and a small smile paints my face,

"You and Daisy Jane are a lot more alike than I thought."

"Me and Daisy Jane are a lot more different than you think too."

"So Jo is out and she ain't waking up anytime soon, wanna stop at the Clubhouse quick."

My head snaps to face him, his eyes are on the road. His elbow on the edge of the window, hand dangling freely, as his other remains stuck on the steering wheel.

"Uhmmm yeah okay," I say it like I mean it. It doesn't really bother me.

We are going to pass the Clubhouse anyway.

Another fifteen minutes and we are parking in one of the three parking bays designated for their cars.

The rest is all for the bikes.

I spot a few Satan Snipers outside their house. They give chin dips and I wave hi as River salutes them jumping out of the car.

The one comes forward and I see it is Killer. The guy is a dream man. A cold deadly one.

"Need you to watch Jo, wanna show Hannah something."

River says it like an order and I expect this guy to refuse but he just leans against the white truck and dips his head.

Wow, okay then.

We walk past the Clubhouse and over a hill. I never knew that the Clubhouse blocked such scenery. I'm wondering where we're going.

River keeps pace ahead of me the entire time. It isn't like I can ask him.

But I see it, the lake, the walking area. It is extraordinary.

I stop just on the hill and take it all in. The number of trees surrounding the other side. The water glistening under the sun's deadly heat. It is all so surreal.

It is like he can hear me because he stops halfway down the hill and faces me.

His face now masked by a seriousness I have come to know as a normal River mask.

I walk down until I stand directly in front of him, my eyes half-dazed,

"Why did you bring me here?" It is words I don't want to know the answer to, but it is that same answer I need.

"I bring Jo here, we sit there." He points to the bank right on the edge of the lake.

"So this is your secret place."

"Yeah, but that isn't why I brought you here." He closes the gap between us, his hand cupping my cheek.

"Oh." It is the only coherent word I think I could say now.

"You once told me that I needed to find my keeper." I start to shake my head already having an idea where this is going.

He slides his finger's behind my neck, and I look into his

blue eyes, "You don't even know me River, that day I gave you something and you didn't even want it. You hurt me."

He drops his rugged face until our foreheads touch, "I have been in love Hannah, I have lost so many people. Fuck, I lost my brother, my own flesh and blood but I have never found a keeper until the day I met you. Over these months I watched you, I got to know you from afar because I knew I wouldn't be able to do it next to you. And baby you are my keeper, maybe it's fucked up because we haven't even spoken much but Hannah give me a fucking chance. Please, I beg you."

I think it's raining but it is just my eyes leaking.

I'm crying, oh gosh I am crying. I nod my head like I'm crazy, saying yes, yes, yes. He kisses me and I swear it is then I know that River is mine.

We sit by the lake until River's phone rings. One call and my man is running up the hill. I don't stop him because whatever it is must be important.

I sit by myself watching the suns lasting rays on the lake waters. Then I walk back up the hill for the first time at peace.

I am not sure where our road would lead. I am not sure whether it will lead in the same direction but I know that we got a good shot.

Killer waits in the driver's seat to take Jo and I home. I get in not wondering, but knowing that River will be there as soon as he can.

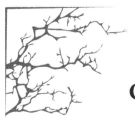

Chapter 12

My life has always been a ride for the finish line. I have watched men bleed until their very souls have twisted and turned, leaving their bodies.

I have seen death in numbers of a thousand. I've faced off with killers who fight for things they know not of.

I have murdered fathers, taken meaningless lives for a country that will never surrender, that will always want more. I have experienced life and love and all those fucking in-betweens'.

I have watched my father die as he took his last breath with so much hate that I wished him to suffer.

Life has always been a fucking ride to the finish line but with my brothers at the back and the throttle of the bike, I have soared breathing in another day.

There is death where I go now. It waits for me, screaming its penance on my sins. I'm choking with the vibration of the engine between my legs.

We ride, as one.

My Kanla brothers having my back. I never thought my life will be this way. I never thought I'll settle for one place. But one we are.

We ride for our souls, we ride for our right, but mostly tonight we ride for our freedom. And we don't fucking stop!

We never slow, this is what we are, this is who we have become chaining ourselves to each other and we do it as one.

People always ask us why do we call ourselves The Satan Snipers.

Today as we unite as one, we conquer, because when we are together it is our enemies we will taint. It is our enemies who will perish.

Tonight, on this day we will spill the blood of the ones who have sinned. We will pass no judgment but the one of a Satan's death. We will be merciless as we punish. We are The Satan Snipers and tonight we will reap vengeance on those who wronged us.

We stop just outside the old broken down warehouse. I line my bike slowing its speed.

It's a clear view of the piece of shit dump. Killer takes his position on my rear as we stop. I pull my helmet off my head and remove my bandana off my face. My knuckles itch for the flesh of my enemy, my heart thumps for the end when we will take our victory.

"It's too fuckin' quiet." Killer hits my shoulder.

"Feels like an ambush. Did you check the fuckin' ammo? I say we go in hot."

"Lemme go in first, there's no need waiting around here." Spade volunteers as fucking always, never met a man who likes a fight more than the brother.

"Killer you and Texas mark the windows. Spade you and Knight go through the front." I stare at Knight when I say this so he knows to watch the brother's back.

I don't fucking need another brother's death on my conscious tonight.

I look at the big meaty brother, Bull who is on my left and rub a hand down my scruff,

"You and I will go through the drain, two meters to the left."

The two women Mercy and After stand in front of me, waiting for my instruction. I can tell by the shake of Mercy's leg that she's itching for a fight,

"You and After will go in first, make it quick and quiet. I want ammo set up in the corners of the block. I got a feeling we going to need a shit load of crap."

"Let's move," I say loud and fucking clear.

After and Mercy duck down, running toward the back.

Texas and Killer go towards the windows.

The rest of us make way to the warehouse. It isn't long before Texas and Killer work out the patrol routine and let Mercy and After know that two of the outfit fuckers patrolling the shit dump have turned their back on the entrance.

Mercy and After crouch down, moving like leopards through the tall grass. Blades ready and thirsty for blood.

I stand guard and watch my people at work. Mercy and After sneak up behind the two fuckers and slit their throats.

I hear the gurgles as their blood flows through their throats like a waterfall. It's a sight of beauty and I get a sick fucking thrill as one of the men clutches his throat, like that, would save him.

No one can save our enemies, not even Satan himself.

They quickly and effortlessly dispatch of the bodies and take them to the side of the warehouse.

That's our queue.

Killer and Texas set their riffles up by the windows. Bull and I head on to the drain while Knight and Spade go in with guns blazing and a fever for the death of our enemies.

I climb down into the drains, Bull following closely behind. The place smells like shit but to us, it's just another fuckin' day at this fucked-upness we call life.

The sound of guns scream through the air as the souls of our enemies become damned to hell.

My feet hit the water as I run through the tunnels.

I pull my gun from my pants, my feet never failing as I draw closer to my people. I cock the gun making sure my bullet is already in the chamber. I hear Bull doing the same.

We get to the other side in the middle of a gun battle.

I sweep my gaze across the floor. There's like four fucking outfit fuckers to one brother.

Some would say we outnumbered, others will convince themselves we crazy but as I lift my gun and point it at one of my enemies I would just tell you that shit just got real.

The guy drops as my bullet meets with the flesh of his forehead.

Knight takes out two more, one with a switchblade through his eye and the other with three bullet holes to his stomach.

After is on the floor with a guy's head between her legs as she squeezes his last breath out of him. Mercy is still standing by the door trigger happy.

I put two more bullets in the guy on my left just for fun as I hear the sound of incoming cars. I don't worry much about it because the Ghost always gets its target.

I go on my search for the person that started it all. For the woman who I was yet to meet.

I go for Beggar.

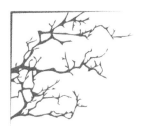

Epilogue

My keeper wasn't one woman, it came in the form of a five-year-old girl. It took me one moment with her to fall in love with the kid and another moment to fall in love with her mother.

Today as I slip this ring on my pregnant wife's hand I bind my keepers to me. My wife once told me that I had to find River's keeper. What she didn't realize was that my keeper came to me.

It all started the day I killed a frog name, Grogg.

Our world is not for the thin blood, it is not for the weak that prey on those weaker.

Our world is for survivors. Whether it be for those who appear fragile yet stand tall. Or for those who crawl.

Our world is for survivors.

For those who had looked death in the eyes and said 'fuck you'.

A year ago I was just a man with a past and present. Today I am a man with a future.

I came back to Kanla to save a girl named Beggar and my journey to find her was one I would always remember as the story behind finding River's keeper.

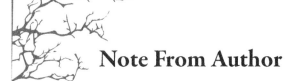

Note From Author

Thank you for reading this novella. River's story was something different. It came to me when I was visiting a retirement village. I met a man, Mr Walters, he was sad, and we eventually started talking. His wife passed on not long before then and I asked how did they meet, he told me a very similar story of what I shared with you guys. The only difference is Mr Walters was a veteran who returned to his home town to sell up his home so he can purchase a farm. The man had no intention of meeting anybody.

The day he met his stepdaughter Neeta, he parked his car in his next door neighbors drive way and bam, he knocked the frog named Grogg.

He fell in love with his stepdaughter after she ripped him a new one, then and there their story began, and 6 months after that he thought if he was going to be in the kids life, might as well be in the mothers too. He married his Marge and though at first they had endless problems, mostly when he told her she was wrong, Mr Walters loved his wife like she could never do a wrong. He told me that sometimes love comes in a different form, might not be what you looking for, but it sure as hell worth holding on to.

He was married for 47 years until his Marge passed on. They had 2 kids after Neeta turned 10. I asked him would he

118

call his story true love? He said it was real love, and his story stayed with me for a while. Upon his passing I decided to write a story similar to Mr Walters in memory of his story.

THANK YOU
    Shan R.K

Don't miss out!

Visit the website below and you can sign up to receive emails whenever Shan R.K publishes a new book. There's no charge and no obligation.

https://books2read.com/r/B-A-DHHG-MEDT

BOOKS 2 READ

Connecting independent readers to independent writers.

Did you love *River's Keeper*? Then you should read *Zero*[1] by Shan R.K!

[2]

Beggar

My fall scattered all the pieces in me until I had a small part left. That last sliver of my humanity was stolen from me by the enforcer of The Satan Sniper's Motorcycle Club. He name is Zero.

Zero

Once Upon a time I met a girl and I loved her with everything in me. Then one day she betrayed me. She chose him over me.

Now she is back but for how long ?

The Satan Snipers continue with their hunt for Lucca as another threat lurks in the misty waters of Kanla.

Women are dying and it is up to The Satan Snipers to find the ones who are guilty.

As the club hunts down their enemies Beggar and Zero are faced with questions and new obstacles in their path.

How do I choose between the woman I love and my own flesh and blood?

Read more at https://shanrk.com.

Also by Shan R.K

Catch Me, If You Can
Shock Me Twice

Liston Hills
School Me Season 1
School Me Season 2
School Me Season 3

Love Hate and Billions
Kylie Bray

Secrets Of The Famiglia
Capo Dei Capi

The Angel Descendants
House Of Legions

The Satan Sniper's Motorcycle Club
Beggar
River's Keeper
Zero
Beauty's Breath

Standalone
Faces Of You

Watch for more at https://shanrk.com.

About the Author

I am a born and bred South African Author.

My passion for writing was not something that suddenly happened. I was born to write words as one is born to die.

My stories are dark and twisted. The Characters are people who we all can relate to.

They are either personas of a certain belief of mine or they are characters portraying the different types of people in our world today.

I love writing fiction and bringing a world alive with words. I believe that a voice is not just one spoken but one seen too.

Since I have started writing I am able to show you that which I wish to scream.

I enjoy reading at any time of day.

My favourite book I have read to date would be Angels blood by **Nilini Singh**. My ATF Author is a definite **Jamie Begley** and my BR series is split between Infernal Devices by

Cassandra Clare and The Black daggerhood brothers by **J.R Ward**.

The longest book I have written to date would go to House of Legions- A paranormal romance about a Lightwatcher and Angel.

The best book I have written would be Beggar - A MC suspense/romance series.

The best idea I have ever had would be to start my blog Liston Hills School me. It is a live online novel I started working on a year ago.

If I could describe myself I would say I am shy but also friendly.

Read more at https://shanrk.com.

Made in the USA
Monee, IL
11 November 2024

69862954R00080